Cashmere
Cries

Dzelda :

Cashmere
Cries

Always Dream BIG! :)

Carmita Daniels

[signature]
4.28.07

KNB Publications, LLC
http://www.knb-publications.com

KNB titles are published by:

KNB Publications, LLC
P.O. Box 831641
Stone Mountain, GA 30083
Email: info@knb-publications.com

KNB Publications, LLC is a Christian Book Publisher dedicated to expanding works that uplift Jesus Christ through the written word. The KNB logo is a registered trademark.

ISBN-13: 978-0-9789702-0-8
ISBN-10: 0-9789702-0-9

First Printing: April 2007

Printed in the United States of America

DEDICATION

To Jesus Christ, who died for my sins so that I may have everlasting life. To my wonderful parents, Arthur and Cinderella Osborn, who gave me the opportunity to have a family; it was an opportunity of a lifetime. I will always cherish the tremendous sacrifices you made for me. I love you, Mama and Daddy. I thank God for blessing me with your unconditional love. Thank you for introducing me to the love of books. Thank you, Mama for being my biggest fan. Thank you for being my rock and my shield. Words can never express my love for you and Daddy.

To my husband, Marcello, who encouraged me to dream big; thank you for loving me past my pain and into my destiny. Thank you for being my confidant, a true gentleman and the man that makes my heart sing. You are my knight in shining armor.

To our beautiful angels, Chatela and Erin, you are God's most precious gifts. I love you both so much. Always reach for the highest stars and remember: Anything is possible if only you believe. Always live life to your greatest potential and never forget the B.I.B.L.E: **b**ountiful **i**nformation **b**efore **l**eaving **e**arth.

Thank you (Granny) Margie Alberta Borders, for being a praying grandmother.

ACKNOWLEDGEMENTS

I can do all things through Christ who strengthens me.
Philippians 4:13

Sharon Ann Borders...I did it! Thanks so much for your inspiration. I love you now and always. I truly appreciate the decisions you made regarding my life. Thank you for allowing Mama and Daddy to raise me. Thank you for giving them the greatest gift...me. You are bone of my bone and flesh of my flesh.

And as for you, father...you know who you are. And I respect your decision to still remain anonymous after thirty-three years. However, I love you regardless.

Chapter 1

Something persuaded Cashmere to just lie in bed, but this particular Sunday, she had been assigned to perform a solo at church. So in spite of being sick the night before, she managed to crawl out of bed, get dressed and arrive at church just in time to jump in line as the choir was preparing to march in.

"Girl, can you zip up my robe?" she asked one of her alto leads as she franticly tried to look together while in fact, she was falling apart.

Cashmere was going through a divorce from the man she had been married to for nine years. For the last six years, the couple had slept in separate bedrooms and for six years, Cashmere had been celibate. In fact, she'd almost forgotten what it felt like to be touched affectionately by a man. Cashmere felt her world falling apart. Even though life with her husband was not a bed of roses, he was the only man Cashmere had ever known intimately. She had waited all of her life to be connected with her soul mate, doing everything according to the Word of God; yet her marriage had failed. In spite of her circumstance, Cashmere always wore an outward smile while crying on the inside.

An attractive woman, standing five feet four inches tall with caramel colored skin, Cashmere mesmerized people with her almond shaped eyes. She was blessed with a perfect hourglass-shaped body frame that screamed sexy, no matter what fabric lined her curves. Men adored her and were naturally drawn to her charm and witty personality. Needless to say, Cashmere was the center of attention when she entered any room. She was an only child and admittedly spoiled, but men desperately wanted to be near her. Anybody that spent any amount of time with Cashmere automatically envied her style and admired her demeanor. Her father nicknamed her Cash when she was born. After the first look at his daughter he knew he would give her anything her heart desired and all that his money could buy. Her father made sure she had a first-class education. From the time she entered kindergarten, Cashmere attended private school at Lakeview Christian Academy and graduated valedictorian of her class. She then enrolled in the University of Georgia where she received a master's degree in law.

Marching down the long aisle of Glory Tabernacle with her fellow choir members, Cashmere's life flashed before her eyes. She had it all: money, a dream house, a luxury SUV, a college degree, stunning beauty, a sweet personality, a loving family and loyal friends. But daily, Cashmere cried, realizing her life was barren and her heart vulnerable.

From the choir stand she looked out into the congregation and saw thousands of smiling faces. She wondered if they were pretending to be happy too.

"Lift up your hands and give God praise; He is worthy-so worthy," Bishop J.T. MacFields proclaimed as he lifted his hands toward heaven. "He is *hoooly*, come on and make a joyful noise unto the Lord," he bellowed, walking across the pulpit. "We need to serve the Lord with gladness: come into His presence with singing, enter into His gates with thanksgiving, and into His courts with praise: be thankful unto Him, and bless His name," he stated calmly as he stood at the podium and flipped through the pages of his Bible. "You may be seated. Turn in your Bibles to Psalm 18. There is a word from the Lord."

2

Cashmere took her seat and flipped through her Bible until she found the book of Psalms. She attempted to read along but in the midst reminders of her dilemma, she lost her concentration.

"I will love thee, O Lord, my strength," Bishop MacFields began, reading from the first verse.

I cannot believe him. How could he treat me this way after all I've done for him? Cashmere thought to herself.

"I will call upon the Lord, who is worthy to be praised: so shall I be saved from mine enemies," Bishop quoted from the third verse.

I gave this man nine years of my life, and for what? Why? she fumed to herself.

"In my distress I called upon the Lord, and cried unto my God: he heard my voice out of his temple, and my cry came before him, even into his ears." Bishop MacFields paused and did not speak for a moment. He rubbed the back of his neck and nodded. "I don't know who I am talking to but God told me to tell you, trouble doesn't last always and He has heard your cries."

Cashmere stopped daydreaming and listened as he continued to quote scriptures from verses nineteen and twenty-one.

"... he delivered me, because he delighted in me. For I have kept the ways of the Lord, and have not wickedly departed from my God." Bishop MacFields closed the Bible and held it close to his chest as he walked back and forth in the pulpit. "I feel in my spirit a wounded soul. You have been abused and mistreated. God knows your deepest needs and He's going to fix it for you. God has heard your cries and because you have been faithful He's going to bless you. God said you may have been delayed but you have not been denied and He's going to reward you for your patience and longsuffering."

Cashmere's eyes welled with tears. Her heart went out to whomever the Bishop was referring to. When the choir director motioned for the choir to stand, Cashmere stood up feeling dizzy, but quickly dismissed the ailment to lead her song. The

3

musicians began to play and the melody ignited her soul. She lived for the moment to sing God's anointed word.

"Praise is what I do... when I want to be close to you...I lift my hands in praise..." Cashmere closed her eyes and sang as if she was serenading God face to face. When she finished her song, there seemed to be not a dry eye in the congregation. Cashmere respected praise and worship. She knew the choir was a ministry and she always prayed that God would use her voice for His glory. Cashmere saturated herself in the anointing of God, then quietly exited the sanctuary. As she felt the stomach pain arise again, she recalled the scripture of Isaiah 53:5.

"But he was wounded for our transgressions, he was bruised for our iniquities," Cashmere recited to herself; "the chastisement of our peace was upon him; and with his stripes *I* am healed, *I* am healed." As she was about to go down the flight of stairs, she felt the presence of someone following her.

"You have the voice of an angel," a deep sensuous voice said from behind. Cashmere looked over her shoulder. "May I?" he asked, reaching out for her hand to escort her down the stairs. "My name is Marcus and I really enjoyed your solo." He held on to her hand like it was a prize trophy.

Marcus was the new church musician, well groomed, extremely handsome with dark chocolate skin like that of an African warrior. Every available woman in the church wanted him but Marcus ignored their advances. Some people thought his solitary behavior was bizarre. Many people questioned his sexuality since he was never seen with a woman. To make matters worse, he received regular manicures and pedicures at the local nail salon. Marcus also owned Beautiful Soft Touch, a new but popular floral company in the heart of town which added to the curiosity of several back-biting people.

"Thank you," Cashmere responded, sounding as nonchalant as she could while looking up at the six foot two inch frame that towered over her body.

"You're quite welcome," he said, gazing profoundly into her eyes. "Tell me your name."

"My name is Cashmere."

Marcus looked intently at every word that left her mouth. "Cashmere...Cashmere..." he whispered to himself in a dreamlike manner. "I finally found you." Marcus spoke the words softly underneath his breath.

"What did you say?" Cashmere said as she gave him a strange glance, pulling her hand away from his.

"Oh, nothing...it was nothing. I was just thinking out loud," Marcus stuttered, still mesmerized by her face.

Cashmere almost laughed. "You shouldn't make a habit of talking to yourself. People may think something is wrong with you."

"I wouldn't have to talk to myself, if I could talk to you. Can I have your telephone number?" Marcus asked, opening the door of the church so that she could exit ahead of him.

Oh here we go again, another tired brother with weak game, she thought to herself as she walked past him and declined his offer. Cashmere was not in the mood for lame pick up lines.

Marcus felt flattered by the challenge as he stood, watching her walk away. He could not help himself as he followed close behind her. In Marcus' opinion, every man loved a good chase, just as long as the woman was worth chasing. And by all means, Cashmere was one of those women he could envision himself thinking about from the time he woke up in the morning until he closed his eyes at night. And even then, she would appear in his dreams.

Marcus had been watching Cashmere for months. He studied and memorized her every move. He knew she licked her lips when feeling nervous. He knew she had a beautiful smile but owned a broken heart. Marcus knew her eyes lit up when she witnessed couples in love. Above all, he knew her name. He had known it for years.

Just as Cashmere reached to open the door to her 2006 Escalade, black and sharp from the inside out, her cell phone rang.

"Hello?"

"Hey Cash."

It was her friend, Melanie. The two had been virtually inseparable since third grade and if secrets had stock, they both would be millionaires. Cashmere and Melanie grew up together and were born only nineteen days apart. Melanie had golden-brown colored skin with dark hazel eyes. She had a voluptuous body paralleled to those of J-Lo and Beyonce. She always styled her hair like famed television arbitrator, Judge Glenda Hatchett, and wore make-up in earth tone colors. Melanie cooked and cleaned on a regular basis and her home was so immaculate that eating off of her floor wouldn't even be considered unsanitary. She used Clorox religiously, as if she received royalties from purchasing the product. Melanie was happily married and always spoke her mind regardless of whose feelings were involved. Cashmere always knew where to turn for the cold hard truth. No matter the situation, she could always count on Melanie to be honest.

"What time should I expect you?" Melanie asked.

"I'm leaving now. Girl, my back is aching and I have the worst stomach ache ever," Cashmere moaned with pain visible on her face.

"Girl, you need to see a doctor, you know there's a bad virus going around in Lithonia."

"Yeah, I heard. Girl, I'll see you in about twenty minutes." Cashmere closed her cell phone and stood for a moment, massaging her belly, trying to relieve the pain in her body that held her hostage. Cashmere's hands began to sweat as the pain increased. Her face was pale and wet as perspiration trickled down the back of her neck. She felt faint and her knees began to weaken, causing her to lose her balance.

"Are you okay?" a voice asked from close behind. It was Marcus. He had broken her fall and held her close against his body. He stared motionless into her face, wiping her face and neck with a handkerchief that he pulled from his pocket. The slight touch of her body made Marcus's world stand still. He was lost in this moment in time.

Oh, dear Lord, have I met a stalker or what? Cashmere said to herself as she studied the intense look on his face.

"I said, are you okay?" Marcus asked again with a fading tone as his breath evaporated from his esophagus.

She nodded. "I'm fine; I just became light-headed all of a sudden."

Marcus saw Cashmere's mouth move and heard the words she'd spoken, but he could not let her go. He was in a deep trance that was accompanied by powerful shock waves that radiated around his heart.

"I'm okay; you can let me go now," Cashmere said, feeling an unmistakable passionate chemistry between them.

"Are you okay, Is there anything I can do?" Marcus's question was sincere as he regained his composure and opened the car door to help her inside. "I want to make sure you are okay," he said while reaching across her lap to fasten her seatbelt.

Cashmere admired his gentle nature. She admired his good looks as well. *Oh, dear Lord, he smells so good.* "I'll be fine," she reassured him as he stepped away and closed the door. Cashmere took one last glance at Marcus before driving away.

Marcus noticed the word "CASH" on her rear license plate. "It has to be short for Cashmere," he said, smiling as he thought of Margie Alberta and the words she spoke to him when he was only thirteen years old.

Chapter 2

Cashmere imagined in her mind how much she truly wanted a knight in shining armor, but she made herself a promise not to get caught up in the idea that Mr. Right existed in this life or the life to come.

Listening to the radio, she heard the words of a familiar love song, *"Always and forever...each moment with you...is like a dream to me that somehow came true..."* The expressions of Luther Vandross pierced through her soul like a fiery hot spear. The words burned deep within her soul as the lyrics said so much about the love she dreamed of.

"Uh, I must change this station," she mumbled. "Love definitely doesn't live here anymore." Nothing on the radio seemed to spark an interest so she popped in *The Rebirth of Kirk Franklin* CD, turned to track number eight, looked in the rear view mirror to check her lip gloss, turned up the volume and sang to the top of her voice, *"Every time I look back...and every time I think back on all the stuff I been through, I prayed through, I cried through and then I tried you..."* Cashmere was driving down Interstate 85 snapping her fingers and bobbing her head to the beat. She was singing from the depths of her soul. After all that Cashmere had been through lately, she needed to hear a motivational song about God's love and mercy.

Upon her arrival at Melanie's condo, the two ladies went out on the balcony for some fresh air and sweet tea. Their conversations about life went as far back as Cashmere could remember. Talking with Melanie brought a sense of appreciation to Cashmere, and for Melanie, it brought a sense of total understanding. As usual, Cashmere had some form of drama in her life. Drama seemed to be a part of her existence, following her everywhere she went. Melanie knew this and accepted the imperfection as would any true friend.

Even though the two had other separate friends, their bond was unique. A friendship not forced or fabricated but two different women with diverse outlooks on life and equal acceptance from both.

"I met the nicest guy at church," Cashmere said. She smiled thinking of how concerned Marcus had been about her. "Girl, he is handsome too."

"They're all nice at first until they get inside our jeans," Melanie stated with a firm look on her face.

"You are right but that's when you fall in love with him first instead of allowing him to be the first to fall in love. Remember, God said a man that finds a woman finds a good thing."

"And how do you allow him to fall in love with you?" Melanie questioned with a raised brow.

"By getting into his head." For emphasis, Cashmere tapped the side of her head with her index finger.

"I don't have time for all those games; either you like me or you don't," Melanie uttered while sipping her tea.

"My point exactly, I don't have time for the games either. That's why I allow the man to play while I pray. In the end either he wins or loses, the choice you make depends on his choices."

"How so?" Melanie inquired.

"Because, if a man really likes you, he will pursue you and study you. He will do whatever it takes to please and accommodate you. He will respect you and honor you. But, if he only wants sex, then he'll eventually slip up and do something stupid and that's your first warning sign to leave him alone," Cashmere said as she winked her eye at Melanie.

"So how do you determine a man's objective from the initial conversation?" Melanie asked.

"Mama always said that within the first three minutes of meeting a man, you can determine what he is all about, but personally, I believe it's in his approach," Cashmere said as she sipped her drink and crossed her legs.

"Go on…" Melanie insisted. "This I have to hear."

"If a man approaches you and the first thing he refers to has anything to do with any part of your body, he's sexually or physically stimulated by you. Many times men seek to have relations instead of relationships. However, if a man approaches you with general conversation then he is interested in what you are thinking."

"You're right," Melanie agreed, not wanting to sound so sarcastic. "Girl you should write a book."

Cashmere giggled at her remark, and then watched while Melanie rose to greet her man.

"Ladies…dinner's ready," Richmond said as he stepped out on the balcony and into the arms of his wife. Richmond Miccoli was a tall man of medium build with a bald head, all of which was sheltered in a deep cocoa complexion. He was attractive, but most women referred to him as a geek. Rich was a bookworm and when he was not working or wooing Melanie, he was at the library. He was financially independent and unlike many men in his income bracket, he was a true gentleman.

Richmond and Melanie met in 2001 while Melanie was employed as a stock broker at AG Edwards & Sons Inc. where Richmond was the investment director. He was fascinated by her sense of humor and sweet personality. As a "good girl who loved bad boys," Melanie, of course, did not share his attraction and barely even noticed him. It was not until three broken hearts later that she decided to give Rich a chance.

Richmond had experienced his share of heartbreaks too. At the time he met Melanie, he was recently divorced from a woman he had been married to for only two years. The marriage ended when Richmond hired a private investigator to follow his ex-wife after he began to notice credit card charges at the Hilton on his monthly statement. This type of infidelity would wreck most men and turn them into vicious dogs, but not Richmond. He became a stronger and better man for the woman who would appear next in his life.

"Thank you baby," Melanie flirted as she brushed against him, kissing his face as if he had just returned from a long business trip.

"Oh, my goodness, can you two love birds stop for a second out of respect for the lonely hearted?" Cashmere whined as she covered her eyes.

"Not a chance!" Richmond announced as he squeezed his wife tighter. "Everyday is our honeymoon!"

"Okay fine, but can you take your lips off her long enough to tell me what's on the menu for today?" Cashmere requested with her hands on her hips.

"Sure. I have prepared T-bone steak, coconut shrimp, loaded baked potatoes, Caesar salad with yeast rolls, homemade lemonade and a sour cream pound cake for desert, so I hope you have a big appetite."

"Yes I do," Cashmere said, almost salivating.

"After you, princess," Richmond said, referring to Melanie. "After you, Cash," he added just before they all went inside to feast on the fabulous meal.

Candles were burning on and around the dinner table. Melanie loved to eat by candlelight and listen to soft jazz. It was nothing out of the ordinary for Richmond to spoil Melanie and Cashmere was happy to be included. The table was set and the plates were prepared, all Melanie and Cashmere had to do was freshen up and enjoy. Just as Richmond had a way with women, he had a way with food. He knew exactly what to do and when to do it without hesitation or instructions. Melanie was the center of his world and she knew it. There was no one that could separate their love. Not in this world or the world to come.

"Thank you love," Melanie said to Rich as he pulled out her chair and scooped her up. His actions were similar to how a parent would do for their child but on this occasion, it was pleasant to observe a man cater to his wife so courteously. Richmond blessed the food and made sure they had everything they needed before he took a bite. It was Richmond's nature to respect women. He was a God-fearing man who honored his vows and insisted on spending quality time with his wife. Rich was a romantic man and extremely thoughtful. He offered the best to his wife everyday of his life. Cashmere fully believed that if Melanie slightly wished for a star, Richmond would find a way to give her the Milky Way galaxy.

"So, how's the food, ladies?" Richmond asked with a charming smile, as if he could not determine the answer by the silence in the room that was only broken to make way for an occasional "Mmm."

"It is lovely Richmond, as always," Cashmere and Melanie said in unison, almost laughing as the two looked at each other, sharing an inside joke. They knew men loved to hear praise; especially Richmond. Melanie understood the importance of praising her husband and in return he cherished her like a precious jewel.

"And how do you manage to cook so well?" Cashmere inquired, falling in love with every bite.

"I learned in military boarding school and in college. Since I was rarely home, I didn't have the luxury of sitting on the kitchen counter watching Mother prepare a meal, or licking batter from the bowl as she made homemade cakes. As boring as it may sound, I actually watched a lot of cooking channels and read a lot of books."

"Books?" Cashmere queried, looking puzzled. "You mean cookbooks?"

Richmond nodded yes as he took a bite of his loaded baked potato.

"Either you are a nerd or just profoundly detailed," Cashmere said jokingly as she bit into a piece of coconut shrimp.

CASHMERE CRIES

"I prefer profoundly detailed," Richmond said, laughing. "What is wrong with a man reading a cookbook? I mean... how else would I have learned? I did not have women beating down my door offering to cook for me. And I definitely could not afford to eat out everyday while I was in college. Not to mention the food was awful in the cafeteria; so I took it upon myself to learn the skill of cooking so I could survive. You have to eat in order to live so why not learn how to do what you need the most? And besides...every woman loves a man who can cook, right?"

"Right baby," Melanie announced as she leaned over to kiss him. "Absolutely right!" she shouted while winking at her man.

Cashmere smiled in appreciation and complete happiness for her friend. While finishing her meal, she had her head in the clouds... If only she had a man so sincere and thoughtful, the last decade of her life would not have been spent in vain. She had wasted nine years of her life catering to a man who did not appreciate the countless positive qualities she brought into the relationship. Cashmere longed for a happy marriage identical to her parents. Growing up, she witnessed their love and affection for one another and tried desperately to walk in their shoes. But with all her attempts, she did not succeed. Now that her preposterous marriage was over, Cashmere was thankful. Her eyes had been opened and she realized her mistake. She had looked at the outward appearance of Donovan instead of looking at his heart.

How could I have been so naïve? So blind, so delusional, she fumed to herself. Cashmere made a decision that from now on, she would not judge the book by its cover. It really wouldn't matter if his nose were too big, teeth crooked, hair too nappy; as long as he had a clean heart. She prayed for unconditional love and a righteous man that would cherish her for a lifetime. In her heart, Cashmere cried for a life filled with sweet joy and ultimate passion. She dreamed of a life not compromised or fake. Cashmere desired a love so unique, that by the look of her countenance, people would know that she was loved. She made

13

an oath to look past the exterior, the finances and all the hype. Cashmere contemplated that she would even look past...

"Girl... what are you thinking about?" Melanie asked abruptly, interrupting her thoughts.

"Nothing," Cashmere said, smiling while finishing her lemonade. "Girl I was somewhere in Fantasyland but I'm back now, I'm back."

Melanie picked up her knife and began cutting her cake. "Please tell me you were not thinking about the man you met at church."

"Who is the lucky fellow?" Richmond asked, smiling at Cashmere as he leaned back in his chair waiting on her response.

"Well... since you put it like that, his name is Marcus," Cashmere said as she winked at Melanie as to emphasize Richmond said "lucky fellow."

Rich leaned forward in his chair, keeping his concerned eyes focused on Cashmere. "How much do you know about Marcus?"

Cashmere sat silently for a moment and pondered Richmond's question. *Now that is the million dollar question of the day. How much do you know about any potential date? In the beginning, they all seem so nice. Don't they? But what happens at the initial stage of dating is total opposite when the real man shows up. You know the one that was hidden on your first date. The one you should have actually met from the start but instead he sent his imposter in order to impress you. And once the ice has been broken, the mask unveiled and abracadabra... the real joker shows up.*

Cashmere could not understand why men lied or tried to impress women with unrealistic ideas of themselves or what they could bring into a relationship. In her experience, men always had a tendency to tell women what they thought she wanted to hear. When it all boiled down to it, the only thing women really wanted was the truth. Any woman who received true information before embarking on a relationship was unlikely to reject a man. Most of the time a man's occupation and financial worth was the last thing considered when a woman imagined Mr. Right.

CASHMERE CRIES

Cashmere remembered when she met Donovan, her soon to be ex-husband, ten years ago. He was a music producer and worked closely with Jermaine Dupree for SO SO DEF Records. He showered her with diamonds and designer labels. Every weekend, he swept her away to an exotic place. He wined and dined her relentlessly, spending thousands of dollars in the process, trying to impress her. Donovan loved Cashmere with his platinum American Express card. He spent money on her instead of spending time with her. Despite everyone else's opinion, Cashmere thought he was the perfect man. It was common for her to be spoiled and enjoy the finer things in life. In her eyes, Donovan was doing nothing out of the ordinary.

After a few short months of imaginary romance, he proposed, they eloped and got married in Rome. Shortly after the honeymoon, he began to change. He pressured Cashmere to sing R&B and to sign a record deal with SO SO DEF, but she refused. Cashmere loved to sing in the church choir and everyone knew she had incredible talent. But singing professionally was never her dream and Donovan resented her from that day forward.

He blamed her. "We could make millions," he would say. "God is not paying you, why are you so committed to that lousy choir?" His words haunted her.

Everything, from the way Cashmere dressed to the places she went, had to change as Donovan demanded she submit unto him. She realized she had been tricked. He became spiteful and irrational, punishing her for his failure to become the next P. Diddy. He wanted to use her talent to make himself famous in the music industry. The nice, kind words he once shared with Cashmere turned into bitter insults. Everything she did to please Donovan was like casting pearls before a swine. He went from worshiping the ground she walked on to burying her self-esteem beneath the earth's surface. She tolerated his nonsense for ten lonely, miserable years; trying time after time to make the relationship work.

Cashmere had prayed and cried out to God many nights for His divine intervention. The more she cried the meaner Donovan became. He refused to touch her and demanded she move permanently into the upstairs bedroom. Cashmere put on a happy face for years but on the inside she shed endless tears. Finally, Cashmere had had enough. She realized Donovan would never change so she filed for divorce. She was financially secure before marrying Donovan Nixon. Along with his income, they shared an annual wage of well over six figures. Money was never an issue, however love and respect was. He never quite understood that all she needed was his fervent affection, not his financial affinity.

Cashmere's silence lingered for a moment longer as she thought in depth about Richmond's question. She was puzzled, yet confident, as she whispered, "Just as much as I knew about Donovan. Absolutely nothing and that's why I am so afraid."

Reality hit her like a truckload of bricks as she excused herself from the dinner table and helped Melanie clear the dishes. Ten years of her life was wasted. And it hurt. Cashmere hid her pain as she loaded the dishwasher for her friend. She hungered for the bond she witnessed between Richmond and Melanie but uncertainty kept her captive. Living a decade-long lie troubled her soul. Cashmere had learned from her mistake and paid dearly for not listening to advice regarding Donovan. She asked God to forgive her for her disobedience and for breaking her marriage vows, but she could not live with Donovan Nixon until death separated them.

Richmond walked over to Cashmere and turned her around so she would be facing him. He took the dish cloth out of her hand and laid it in the sink so that he could hold her hands inside his as he looked at the hurt and disappointment on her face.

"Cash, you are a beautiful woman inside and out. A man would be a fool not to cherish you," Rich said, genuinely concerned.

"He's right," Melanie said, as she placed her arm around Cashmere to comfort her.

Richmond released Cashmere's hands and then held her face in the palms of his hands. "Cashmere, you are any man's dream and don't you ever think differently."

"Yeah girl, you're all that and a snack," Melanie teased, as she rubbed her hand up and down Cashmere's back, trying to conjure up a smile from her best friend.

Cashmere's heart was heavy as she failed to fight back the tears. In the midst of all her turmoil, she believed that God had heard her cries. She remembered the sermon and she recalled the voice of Bishop J.T. MacFields saying, "I don't know who I am talking to but God told me to tell you, trouble doesn't last always and He has heard your cries."

Chapter 3

On most Monday mornings, Cashmere would have already headed for the nail salon to get a pedicure, but this particular morning she opted to meet Olivia at the local high school to walk the track. She hoped to burn away the extra calories she consumed over the weekend from the scrumptious meal Rich had prepared.

"Now I hope she's on time and I pray to God she does not start talking about how much weight she imaginarily lost," Cashmere said, grabbing a water bottle from the passenger seat.

Olivia is one of those people who dieted unsuccessfully by expecting ten pounds to miraculously disappear after completing a two mile walk. Her favorite line was, "I've lost ten pounds, can you tell?" And of course, the person the question was directed toward would have to agree just to appease Olivia and keep her motivated. Cashmere did not want to hear any nonsense regarding instant weight loss this morning.

After one last check of her lip gloss, Cashmere climbed from her SUV and closed the door. As she approached the area that was automatically her and Olivia's starting point, she noticed Olivia coming around the track, finishing a lap.

She just be a-marchin' like goin' to war. A clip from *The Color Purple* entered Cashmere's mind. Olivia was swinging her arms just like Sophia, in the scene where she and Harpo were going to see Mister. She could not help but compare the two scenes as Olivia rounded the track kicking up dust.

"Hey Sophia," Cashmere said with a country accent, almost bursting into laughter at her own joke.

"What?" Olivia asked huffing, unaware of what Cashmere was talking about.

"Nothing." Cashmere shook her head, trying to hide her laughter. "I see you started without me. How many laps have you walked?" Cashmere asked, while bending over to do a few stretches to loosen her muscles. Olivia stopped to tie her shoelace, and then rested her hands on her hips as she waited for Cashmere to finish her squats.

Olivia was a gorgeous woman with toffee-colored skin that was as smooth as silk. She had long wavy hair, the type most women paid to have weaved or sewn in. By the looks of her thick mane you would naturally assume that her heritage included Indian. Olivia was full figured and although she lugged an extra ninety pounds on her five foot six inch body frame, she wore the latest fashions and hottest trends. Her motto was: "I have a weight problem. My weight problem does not have me." Olivia was devoted to God and was blessed with a powerful angelic voice.

The two, along with Melanie, had been friends since grammar school. Olivia had a heart of gold and always went out of her way to help others.

"Only three and I'm tired already," Olivia said, breathing heavily. "What took you so long? I was beginning to think you were not coming."

"I stopped by the bank to make a deposit and while I was there, I ran into Marcus, the new musician at our church," Cashmere said, trying to hide the huge smile on her face.

"Ooooh, you like him…" Olivia playfully taunted.

"He seems nice," Cashmere replied in a tone as nonchalant as she could muster.

"Is his last name Davenport?" Olivia inquired, trying to piece together information.

"I don't know, I never asked."

"If his name is Marcus Davenport, I heard he's really nice and handsome too. And he owns a floral shop, I heard someone say." Grilling for more information Olivia asked, "Does he sing with a gospel group?"

"I have no idea. I said I bumped into him, not read his biography," Cashmere said.

Olivia lived a simple life but she had more news and information than channels two, five and eleven. She could even give CNN a run for their money. Cashmere always teased her by telling her she'd missed her calling as a news reporter or private investigator. She even called Olivia "Detective O" from time to time, telling her that she put the "N" in nosey and the "C" in curious.

"You are not funny," Olivia frowned, pursing her lips and shaking her head.

"Well, you're asking me questions I cannot answer."

"Okay, fine; answer this…you like him don't you?" she asked once more, staring into Cashmere's face.

Do I like Marcus? Mmm, that seemed like a trick question, Cashmere thought to herself as she tried to process Olivia's probing question. She knew that she needed to respond before her silence conjured up more inquiries. "I had a brief conversation with Marcus as I left church on Sunday. He asked for my telephone number but I did not give it to him. I have too much to resolve with Donavon before I can entertain the thought of another man," Cashmere told her, as she stopped to drink from her water bottle.

"When will the divorce be final?" Olivia's voice was glossed with concern.

"Not long now…not long at all," Cashmere uttered with a sigh of relief.

"Have you spoken with Donovan?"

"No, there is no reason to. The divorce details were pretty painless. We were in agreement when it came to resolving our assets, which made it easy for both our attorneys."

"No regrets?" Olivia pried, waiting for a response.

"Definitely no regrets," Cashmere confirmed with a solid look in her eyes. "None whatsoever." The only regret Cashmere had was marrying Donovan. She refused to listen to her father who had warned her that Donovan was not the man for her. He pleaded with her to wait but Cashmere had already jumped the broom.

Olivia slowed her vigorous pace down to a stroll. She wanted to make sure Cashmere heard every word she spoke. "You made the right decision by trying to make it work with Donovan, even though he defiled you in every way. You did your part as a wife. It did not work, but it is not your fault. At least you can walk away with a clean conscious knowing you did all you could to save the marriage."

"Amen, sister. I didn't give up and throw in the towel like most women would have," Cashmere murmured. "I fought a long hard fight."

Olivia grabbed Cashmere's arm and lifted it in the air. "And you're the champion," she announced, embracing her friend. "You hold the title to your life and the key to unlock your destiny."

"I know," Cashmere uttered. "I look forward to a new beginning."

The two walked in unison around the track, occasionally stopping to wipe sweat from their foreheads and drink from their water bottles. The best exercise for Cashmere and Olivia was an hour of brisk walking. It was the perfect opportunity to release stress and at the same time, talk to God.

"Just keep an open mind, you never know what God has in store for you," Olivia suggested.

Cashmere looked at her from the corner of her eye, promptly raising an eyebrow. "Meaning?"

Olivia took a deep breath and stopped suddenly. "What do you really think of Marcus? You must have made quite an impression on him if he asked for your phone number so quickly."

Not this again, Cashmere thought. If stares could burn holes into people, Cashmere's glare would have burned a tunnel into Olivia's face. The more she thought the more she came to the conclusion that Olivia was not going to let the questions rest regarding Marcus. *She is dead set on interrogating me today.* Olivia was forcing Cashmere to open up and identify with her true feelings. Cashmere remembered how Marcus treated her so delicately. *Not to mention he smelled so doggone good.*

"He's cute, I guess." Instantly, Cashmere knew she had told a little white lie. She took another sip from her water bottle as she withdrew her last statement. "As a matter of fact, he's down right fine, girl!" After the outburst, Cashmere regained her composure and lowered her tone. "I'm so scared of being betrayed again. Mama always told me good men are few and far between."

"You deserve to be in a healthy relationship," Olivia said, trying to encourage her friend.

Cashmere tapped Olivia on the shoulders. "You deserve a good man too."

"Yeah, I know; but I'm just so fat." Olivia looked down at her full figure frame with sadness in her eyes.

"Girl, you need to stop thinking so negatively. There's a man out there for you and in due time, he'll come and he will love you just the way you are, inside and out," Cashmere reassured her. "And besides, what man in his right mind could resist such a gorgeous face?"

A tiny tear flowed down Olivia's smooth velvet skin as she let out a deep sigh. "You're just saying that, Cash."

"No I am not. Look, you are not the only big girl in the ATL. When God sends you a mate, he will love you just the way you are. If you would get out of the house you will see that there are men that love full-figured women. Some men do not like skinny women. I've always heard, 'Nobody wants a bone but a dog.'

You would be considered a goddess if you lived in the Caribbean, around St. Thomas and those parts. I hear they love big women. In fact it's a reflection of your wealth and status."

"Well, I don't have any plans on going there to get my groove back," Olivia said jokingly.

"You sure about that, Stella?" Cashmere teased.

Olivia nodded her head. "I'm sure."

"I just want you to appreciate the talent you have. Most people would kill for a voice like yours. Stop looking at the exterior and focus on the interior," Cashmere said in a convincing manner. "Look at it this way. If you were a man shopping for a vehicle, would you purchase a car that was newly painted with shiny rims but the motor and transmission were no good, or would you purchase a vehicle that had a few dents in the bumper with cheap hub caps but the motor and transmission were brand new?" Cashmere quoted her food for thought.

"Okay, you made your point. I get it now," Olivia said with a broadened smile.

Cashmere raised her eyebrow. "Good because for a second there I thought you had lost your mind."

"And the devil is a lie," Olivia responded spiritually.

"Amen," they said in unison, giving each other high fives in the process.

"What do you have planned to do on your big day?" Olivia asked.

"Divorce Donovan," Cashmere said, trying not to crack a smile.

"You are so crazy," Olivia teased. "I don't know what I am going to do with you. You are something else."

The two shared a laugh and a hug as they climbed the many steps that led to their cars.

"Just wait," Olivia said as she stepped inside her champagne colored Navigator. "The Bible says a man that finds a wife finds a good thing."

"And I knooooow… I am a good thing," Cashmere called out over her shoulder as she climbed into her SUV.

23

"My, my, my… how we toot our own horn," Olivia taunted as she began her ignition.

"Beep, beep," Cashmere sang, tooting the horn of her vehicle twice to coincide with her melodically chanted words.

Chapter 4

It was after eleven o'clock a.m. when Cashmere arrived at her home. She quickly undressed, lit her favorite candles and poured honey shea bubble bath into her huge custom made black marble tub. She tested the water and it was hot, just the way she loved it. Cashmere reached above her head to turn on the wall mounted plasma television to watch the last twenty-five minutes of *The View.*

"Star looks amazing," she gasped as she slipped into the hot bubbly water. *My, my, my...what a high-quality man will do to a woman's image, weight, dreams and attitude. And check out that rock.* "You go girl!" Cashmere shouted while looking into the screen.

In Cashmere's opinion, when Mr. Right came along, women tended to dress differently, lose a few extra pounds, take special care of their skin, hair, nails and especially their feet. She was convinced that women went through a lot of changes to impress a man, but Cashmere wondered what changes a man bothered to go through while trying to impress women. She honestly could not think of anything, especially when she looked back on her relationship with Donovan. *It's time for men to step up to the plate and more importantly, it's time men start batting home runs.*

Cashmere finished her bath, grabbed a towel from the towel warmer, and walked into her closet to rub cocoa butter balm all over her body. Just as she stood to reach for her robe, the doorbell rang.

"Now who on earth could this be? I do not like unexpected company," Cashmere fussed to herself as she ran downstairs to open the door.

"I have a special delivery for *you*, Cashmere Nixon," said a tall man dressed in a blue uniform and sporting a matching cap.

Cashmere wondered how the man, who she did not know, knew that the name on the package was hers. Just because she answered the door didn't mean that she was Cashmere Nixon, but his words had sounded so certain. Cashmere dismissed the thought from her mind as quickly as it had developed as she gazed at the package in his hand.

"Someone must really be enchanted by you," the delivery man added just before leaving Cashmere to herself to inspect the package.

Covering her mouth, she could not believe her eyes. "Oh my goodness." Cashmere was in shock as she took the two-dozen yellow long-stemmed roses into her foyer. She quickly found a vase to house her flowers and sat down on the living room floor and read the enclosed card:

Cashmere,

Please accept these roses as a small token of my sincere hopes of becoming better acquainted with you. I would like to treat you to a special dinner tonight. Please do not allow my proactive behavior to scare you. I am a hopeless romantic; a simple man with a huge heart. Join me tonight at The Sundial. Our reservations are at 7pm. I look forward to conversing and sharing dinner with you.

Sincerely,
Marcus

26

CASHMERE CRIES

Even though the roses were magnificent and the gesture was extremely kind, Cashmere declined Marcus's invitation. The journey to mental and emotional stability had been a long one, and she was not ready to accept any type of romance in the near future. During the process of the divorce, she intended to find herself and heal as Rich had after his bitter break up.

As she lifted herself from the floor, she inhaled, taking one last whiff of the roses before preparing to go upstairs to get dressed. "Thank you Marcus, this was very sweet of you," Cashmere whispered to herself as she stood looking at the amazing floral arrangement that graced her coffee table so beautifully. "However, I apologize but I cannot join you tonight; please forgive me."

More than anything, Cashmere wanted to dash upstairs and put on her favorite black Channel dress with the matching stiletto shoes and purse. She desired to lightly mist her body with Poeme perfume and comb her hair away from her face to show off her eyes, but she could not accept Marcus's invitation no matter how appealing it seemed. In all honesty, Cashmere could not stand another disappointment or heartbreak in her life. The idea that Marcus could be another jerk outweighed her belief that he could really be a nice guy.

Cashmere tossed aside the romantic ideas that raced through her head. She turned her eyes away from the roses, shrugged her shoulders and mumbled in disappointment, "Maybe some other time, Marcus."

Cashmere needed someone to talk to but she did not want to burden anyone with her very personal and private issues. She could always count on her parents when she needed guidance or a listening ear; however, her parents lived in Hawaii and that made it difficult for her to have an immediate shoulder to cry on.

Mr. and Mrs. Osborn loved and truly missed Cashmere, who was their only daughter. Growing up in the Osborn's home gave Cashmere the greatest experience in life. Love, stability, morals and dreams were just a few of the qualities they instilled in their daughter at a very tender age. They taught Cashmere to love

God, to appreciate her own existence and to always respect her body, as it was God's gift to her.

Mr. Osborn received an opportunity to expand his construction company in Hawaii six years ago and since January of 1999 they had been pleading with Cashmere to join them in Waikiki. Even though she had visited her parents regularly, along with calling three times a week, Atlanta was Cashmere's home.

"I need a drink," Cashmere murmured while fiddling with her hair. She knew the exact spot she could go to escape her gloom. She rushed upstairs, threw on her Bebe hat, t-shirt, and jeans and headed for the nearest Starbucks.

"How may I assist you today?" asked the girl at the counter.

"I would like a medium vanilla latte, please," Cashmere answered slowly, contemplating getting a large cup, but deciding the medium would do just fine.

As she looked inside her wallet for money; Cashmere discovered a small blue box that took her attention away from the cashier that stood in front of her. Inside the box was the 3.5 carat diamond ring that Donovan presented when he proposed to her over a decade ago. After staring at the box for a short time, Cashmere anxiously put it away, paid for her drink and left as quickly as she arrived. Bringing back old memorabilia at this stage in her life was useless. Picking up her cell phone to call Olivia, she answered an unexpected incoming call instead.

"Cash, hi, this is Taylor. Your jewelry is ready for pick-up anytime you're ready."

"Okay, thanks girl. I'll be there in ten minutes."

As Cashmere closed her cell phone, she could not stop thinking about Marcus. Even though she was scared and had serious apprehensions about moving forward with a new relationship, there was just something very charming and unique about his demeanor that she could not quite identify. From the initial conversation, he had an exceedingly familiar spirit that was warm, inviting and as strange as it may seem…he felt safe.

CASHMERE CRIES

✳ ✳ ✳ ✳ ✳

"Welcome to Taylor's. How may I help you?" asked a well-groomed middle age lady who appeared to be in training.

"I am here to see Taylor."

"You must be Mrs. Nixon," she acknowledged. "I've heard so much about you. I'll let Taylor know you're here. Please come with me to the VIP room and I'll serve you a refreshing drink," she offered kindly, while she escorted Cashmere into a plush room.

"I'm fine; I just had a drink from Starbucks, but thanks for offering."

"Okay, well since you're comfortable, I'll go get Taylor," she said, smiling as she backed out of the doorway.

Cashmere had attended The University of Georgia with Taylor. They met in the campus bookstore on the day of registration and later found out that they were roommates. The two women had a lot in common, both spiritually and emotionally. Taylor's heart had been shattered during her adolescent years when her parents divorced. Her father and his mistress were the reasons for the severing of her parents' marriage. Taylor vowed to never love a man as long as she had breath in her body. She went through high school and college without ever having a boyfriend. She put all of her energy into her education and her diamond business. Now, Taylor was thirty-two years old but didn't look a day over twenty-one. She had long black hair, round innocent eyes and a flawless figure. Natural beauty was her forte, with lip gloss being the only cosmetic she'd ever had to purchase.

Cashmere looked around the room, remembering the countless times she had spent with Mr. Nixon in the VIP room. With all the thousands of dollars Donavon had spent on diamonds, he demanded she bring them in for a cleaning and prong check twice a month. On evenings that she would accompany him at important dinner engagements, he demanded she bring her diamonds in for cleaning beforehand. Not that they needed to be cleaned that often, but because he wanted to make sure he impressed his business partners, Donovan wanted everything on Cashmere's body to be perfect, including her diamonds.

"Hey Cash, you're all set," Taylor said, walking in and handing Cashmere her usual blue velvet case filled with diamond necklaces, rings, bracelets and earrings, sparkling as bright as the sun.

"They all look amazing, thanks so much," Cashmere said while putting her box away in the complimentary tote bag.

Taylor looked radiant, as usual. Cashmere often wondered why she worked or even made phone calls to clients. *She could be on an island somewhere; Lord knows the girl is loaded.* It was no secret to Cashmere that Taylor owned three diamond companies in the metropolitan Atlanta area; one in Lithonia, another in Alpharetta and the third was located in Sandy Springs.

"You're welcome. You know I have to take special care of my favorite client," Taylor replied.

"You're so successful, why do you work so hard?" Cashmere finally verbalized the question she'd inwardly pondered often.

"Girl you know how I am, I don't trust people, especially with my money; so I keep a strong eye on all my stores."

The two shared many laughs and talked for quite some time. Taylor was successful but she had not let go of the past. She still despised her father and the entire male species.

The shared conversation between the women was briefly interrupted when Taylor received a business call on her cell phone and quietly excused herself.

Once alone, Cashmere spent the time reminiscing on all the extravagant times she shared at Taylor's with Donovan. Even when she only glimpsed at her life, Cashmere's heart felt heavy. Donovan had spent a great deal of money on material possessions when all she ever wanted was unconditional love which was entirely free of charge. It took her a while, but Cashmere had finally come to realize that she had only been a trophy wife for his business purposes only.

Taylor returned to the room, breaking Cashmere's brief reflection. "I'm sorry; I had to take that call. I'm planning on opening another store in Buckhead in the beginning of next year."

"I am so happy for you," Cashmere said, embracing her friend.

"We have to get together soon. I know your birthday's in a few days. I have to leave out Wednesday and I will not be back in town for two weeks…" Taylor's voice faded and then she continued. "So I'll call you when I return. We can get together for dinner or maybe a day at Chateau Élans spa. My treat."

"It's a date."

"Come on, let me walk you out," Taylor offered, leading the way.

On her way out Cashmere noticed a young man, approximately twenty-one years old, talking with a salesman about purchasing an engagement ring for his sweetheart. It captivated Cashmere's attention to see him openly express his love. It touched her heart in a way that made tears fall from her eyes. She listened attentively and was touched by his words.

"I love my girlfriend so much but five thousand two hundred dollars is not in my budget for an engagement ring," the young man said with a distraught look on his face.

"Just think of it this way, she'll love you for life with this rock," the salesman replied with a tone of professional influence.

The love-struck gentleman scratched his head. "Well, she'll have to love me on a fifteen hundred dollar budget. I have been saving my pennies since high school to purchase her a ring but I had no idea they were so expensive. Trust me, she's one in a million and I will spend a million years trying to give her the best, but for now I simply cannot afford this ring. Please show me something in a lower price range."

The salesman nodded. "Okay, no problem, I understand; follow me please."

As Cashmere continued to listen to the heartfelt words spoken by the young shopper, she felt a tingle in her soul. He

31

told the salesman that he had dated his girlfriend since tenth grade and they both had graduated from Georgia State University. He said their college years were difficult because both their fathers were killed in a car accident and their mothers had not smiled until he told them about his plans to propose. In high school, he made a commitment with his girlfriend to practice abstinence until their wedding night. Cashmere believed his character was phenomenal and she knew the diamond he chose would be a genuine token of his love instead of just a show piece.

"Taylor," Cashmere whispered to her friend, pulling from her purse the same little blue box that had upset her at Starbucks. "Would you clean this ring for me please and put it in a new box?" she asked very quietly, trying to be inconspicuous.

"Sure, I'll be right back." Taylor smiled as she had been watching and listening to the same conversation. She knew Cashmere was a hopeless romantic and loved to witness couples in love.

Cashmere stood from afar and continued to admire the young man's personality. Closing her eyes, she said a silent prayer for their pending marriage. *Dear God, please allow this young man to love his wife unconditionally. Give him the knowledge of what she needs and desires. Allow them precious moments to spend together to renew their love daily and most of all God please keep their spirit as new and alive as it is today. Amen.*

After a short while, Taylor returned with a look of anticipation on her face. She placed the box in Cashmere's hand without saying a word. She knew her friend all too well.

"Thank you Taylor," Cashmere whispered and smiled, winking her eye. Taking the box, she walked over to the young man, bit her bottom lip, and with apprehension said, "Excuse me; I could not help but to overhear your conversation. I admire your love for your girlfriend and I find it amazing that both of you practiced abstinence while dating. I know that God will bless your marriage." Cashmere reached out and placed the small blue box in his hand. "Please accept this gift."

The young man was unable to adequately express his thoughts when he opened the box and saw the stunning diamond. His mouth dropped open as he stared at Cashmere in disbelief. "Uh, ma'am, are you sure?" He shuddered. "I mean, why, uh… I just can't believe this is happening. I am speechless."

"Just make your bride-to-be happy and keep your wedding vows close to your heart," Cashmere was near tears as she spoke. "Take this ring, bless it and ask your girlfriend for her hand in marriage."

"How can I ever repay you?" he asked. "How?"

She took his hand and looked deep into his pleading eyes. "When you are married, love your wife from the crown of her head to the soles of her feet." Cashmere accepted the firm, heartfelt embrace from the man who made a vow to her that he would love his wife-to-be eternally, and then she walked away with contentment in her heart.

Chapter 5

November 9th was not only Cashmere's birthday, but the day that would mark the beginning of her new life. A chapter in her life was finally coming to a close and she would no longer be Mrs. Nixon. Though she thought her marriage would be forever, and she had done everything possible to make it so, the idea of being single exhilarated her mind. She knew divorcing Donovan would be a highlight in her life. She had thought of many ways to celebrate, but divorcing him was a celebration in itself. Cashmere was confident that she had exhausted every effort to salvage their marriage. However, some things needed to be disposed of and this counterfeit marriage was at the top of her agenda. For the last ten years of her life, she had been holding on to a relationship that was emotionally null and void.

"All rise," the bailiff instructed as he stood straight as an arrow and stiff as a board. He appeared to be in his late seventies and had the mannerisms of a Sergeant Major. Cashmere wondered to herself, *Why do old men serve as security in a tense judicial court system? Lord knows if anything happens there would be nothing they could do.*

"The honorable Judge Todd Walker will preside in the above matter of Nixon vs. Nixon," he said with a stern but shaky voice. "You may be seated."

CASHMERE CRIES

Just as Cashmere took her seat, she noticed the look in Donovan eyes. He seemed to have so much hatred in his heart. She began to ask herself how she could have married such a cold-hearted man. She had tried everything to be a perfect wife. Cashmere gave him her all, leaving no stones unturned. She made sure he was well taken care of in spite of the fact that he treated her so badly. Cashmere recalled the countless times that she had laid out his clothes for him, along with his shoes and socks. She even looped his belt through his belt loops in addition to spraying cologne on his shirt. In the evenings, he would come home to a bubble bath with a clean towel and washcloth on the sink. She mounted toothpaste on his toothbrush and poured mouthwash in his cup. Many times she purchased Donovan new pairs of silk boxers. Cashmere cooked and cleaned consistently. To be honest, she treated him like a king and he never even said thank you. After all she had done for the selfish idiot he had the audacity to give her an evil look. She knew he hated her for not singing R&B but Cashmere knew God gave her the talent to sing, and she would use her voice to praise God and God only. At that moment, Cashmere forgave him and her conscious was free. It was her big day and she would not carry the weight of Donovan Nixon on her back any longer.

"It is my understanding that both parties have mutually agreed to divide all marital assets and to dissolve the marriage union between Mr. and Mrs. Nixon due to irreconcilable differences. Is that the accurate testimony of both clients?" asked the honorable Judge Walker.

"Yes your honor; that is correct. Both parties are in agreement, therefore, we may proceed," her attorney stated as Donovan's attorney amicably agreed, motioning his approval to Judge Walker.

"Then it is so ordered as previously agreed to by both parties involved that Mrs. Nixon retains sole ownership of the property located at 1839 Chateau Estates. The 2006 Escalade shall also remain the personal property of Mrs. Nixon as well as the vacation home in Hawaii. The six hundred seventy-nine thousand dollars in the savings account shall also be awarded to Mrs. Nixon. Mr. Nixon shall have sole possession of the time share property in St. Maarten as well as the 2006 Hummer H2. It is also prearranged that Mr. and Mrs. Nixon equally divide the eight hundred ninety four thousand dollars in the checking account and Mrs. Nixon shall also re-establish use of her maiden name Osborn as requested in the divorce decree. This divorce shall be final after all papers are signed," ordered Judge Walker as he slammed the gavel down with a loud thump. "Court's adjourned."

Cashmere felt an urge to break-dance into a hallelujah praise shout, but instead, she proceeded to leave the courtroom in the same manner in which she arrived; with her composure. She definitely did not want a confrontation with Donovan. She elected to leave all the pain behind as she trotted down the courtroom steps. Cashmere was determined to leap into her new life with no bitterness or afterthought.

Chapter 6

Cashmere had taken a lengthy vacation to Hawaii to spend time with her parents. She loved every minute of being in their presence. It was an opportunity for her to heal and rediscover herself on a whole new level.

Taylor had flown in to spend the last week with Cashmere in her vacation home. They shopped until their feet could take no more walking, enjoyed fine dining and spent many hours in the spa, pampering the feet they'd overused. The friends felt like new women. They inspired each other to give life and love another chance. For the first time in her life Cashmere witnessed Taylor flirting back with a man.

It had been a few weeks since Cashmere had spoken to Melanie or Olivia, with the exception of an occasional email. In reading her latest email from Melanie, Cashmere learned that Melanie was helping Rich research his family tree. He was just that type. Always learning and discovering. Rich and Melanie wanted so desperately to have a child but before they made any attempt to conceive, Rich wanted to find his birth mother and father. They were a fairly healthy couple but neither wanted to chance a genetic mishap. Rich began research nearly a year ago. He started in his hometown of Vivian, Louisiana but was unsuccessful. He had spent the majority of his life in military boarding schools and college so his knowledge of the people of his hometown was limited. The few people he knew had either moved away or were deceased. Richmond's investigation became tiresome and completely exhausting.

"Rich, we may need to rethink our concept of having a baby. I know you are trying to find your parents but this may prolong our conception indefinitely," Melanie said, looking at the weary face that belonged to her husband.

This issue had almost drained them both mentally and emotionally. Looking into the past brought back many unanswered questions and it showed on Rich's face. He wanted desperately to find his biological parents. He imagined what their faces looked like. He wondered how their voices sounded. He questioned his existence. He questioned whether he had been conceived out of love or a one night stand. But when he observed the frustration in his wife's face, Richmond forgot about himself.

"We've been at this for a long time," Melanie said, staring into space.

"I know baby, but I really can't give up now," Rich said, leaning over to massage her shoulders. "We have to have patience. I have prayed to God without ceasing. I don't believe He brought me this far to leave me."

Melanie reached up to put her hand on top of his and then looked him in the eyes. "Okay, but my biological clock is ticking,"

"I will not keep you waiting any longer than necessary. I want a baby just as much as you. I cannot wait to create life with you and to watch our love grow for nine months inside your womb. Baby, let me check one last thing," Richmond said as he bent down to kiss Melanie on the lips.

"Promise?"

"Promise," Rich vowed, holding her tight.

Rich had never broken a promise to Melanie and he was not about to start. All of his attempts to locate his biological family had failed, but Rich was determined to find answers. His brain literally ached but he refused to be defeated. He wanted Melanie to be proud of him. He never wanted her to see him fail.

For hours, Richmond sat in his home office contemplating his next move. He flipped through his Rolodex, but found nothing. He tried searching the internet but that too, was unproductive. Rich leaned back in his chair and inhaled deeply as his eyes roamed around the room. He focused on a blue book with silver lettering on the hardback jacket. It was his yearbook from Riverside Central Military Academy. Finding new inspiration, Richmond jumped up and ran over to the bookcase, almost knocking over his desk organizer in the process. He grabbed the book and blew dust off the cover as he scrambled back to his desk. Opening the book, Rich's eyes scrolled over the signed autographs and farewell wishes his former classmates had written. He hoped something would help him find his past. He was about to close the book when he noticed a message on the back inside flap. It was from Michael and it read:

Rich,

When you really become Rich; look a brother up in Oil City, LA.

Peace,
Michael Harris

"Yes," Rich shouted, throwing his hands up in the air. "Yes!" he shouted for the second time, so excited that he nearly flipped himself out of the chair. Trying to regain his composure Rich reasoned within himself that he had to control his emotions. Nothing was promised but at least now, there was hope.

Both Michael and Richmond had been enrolled in the same military boarding school since their elementary years. They'd had a few classes together and played on the same football team. They were not best friends but they mingled on occasion to "shoot the breeze." They were the only two in the school that had been born and raised in Louisiana, which made it easy for them to relate to each other. Richmond knew that Oil City was only ten miles from Vivian, and between those small towns, surely there was a nosey person in the midst. He decided to give Michael a call. Perhaps his former classmate had the information he needed. Rich dialed information and sure enough, there was a Dr. Michael Harris listed in Oil City, Louisiana.

Rich wrote the telephone number in his rolodex and leaned back in his chair, breathing a sigh of relief. Praying silently, he took another deep breath, and dialed Michael's telephone number. Two rings later, he'd made a successful connection.

"Hello. Dr. Michael Harris."

"Hello, Michael. This is Richmond Miccoli. We attended Riverside together."

"Of course; I remember you. How are you doing?"

"I'm doing fine," Rich said nervously.

"Are you Rich yet?" Michael teased, remembering what he had written in Richmond's yearbook.

The recall was simple, but somehow it relaxed Richmond and he and Michael talked for hours. During the lengthy conversation, Rich found out that Michael was a doctor at Caddo Memorial Hospital and Michael's mother, Elizabeth, had been a labor and delivery nurse for thirty-two years. Vivian was a very small town where everybody knew everybody and their business, especially Elizabeth Harris. She knew every child that had been born at Caddo Memorial and every mother that had given birth.

Michael's father passed away after suffering a stroke when Michael was three years old. Elizabeth knew she could not raise a boy to be a man so with much contemplation, she decided on sending him to a military boarding school. After her husband's passing and Michael's going away for schooling, she did not have an interesting life. This led her to over-indulge in other people's business. If there was any gossip, Elizabeth knew the beginning, middle and ending. The local people in town referred to her as *the informant*. Many people would joke and say Elizabeth knew the news before it aired on television.

Chapter 7

"**T**here's no place like home," Cashmere said, pulling into the driveway of her house. She parked her Escalade and then ran around to the rear of it. Even though it was the first week of December, the sun was bright and the temperature was similar to a warm summer day. She could barely carry the luggage and souvenirs she brought from Waikiki.

Cashmere unlocked the door and rushed inside to begin unpacking from her long vacation. But first, she sat down on the sofa to catch her breath. Her eyes scanned the place; everything was just the way she left it. Cashmere had enjoyed her time away, but she missed her friends and decided to give Melanie a call. Her purse and cell phone were outside in the SUV, so Cashmere used her hands to push herself off the sofa and at that very moment, a pain hit her left side and she fell to her knees and then to a fetal position. It was an aching she had never felt before, moving from the left side of her body to the right and back again as if someone was cutting her flesh with a double-edged sword. Cashmere wanted to cry out for help but the pain left her immobile and unable to find her voice. As she felt herself beginning to slip in and out of consciousness, she whispered The Lord's Prayer and the 23rd Psalm.

CASHMERE CRIES

❋ ❋ ❋ ❋ ❋

Marcus stood at the counter of the floral company that he owned. He had stopped by to bring Krispy Kreme donuts to his employees and to gather bank deposits. All he could think about was Cashmere as he studied the billboard that read Beautiful Soft Touch. He hadn't seen her in weeks and he was sickened by her absence. Church had not been the same without her presence. He missed her tremendously from the choir stand. Marcus had not heard a response from her since he, disguised as a delivery man, had personally delivered the two dozen yellow long stem roses to her front door. *She did not even look me in the face.* Marcus sighed at the depressing thought. Nor did she accept his offer. He wondered if he had been too assertive. After careful consideration, he decided to send her an apology in the mail.

Dear Cashmere,

I know it has been a while since we last spoke and I know you did not accept my invitation to dinner. Please accept my apology and I...

Before Marcus finished writing the letter he ripped the paper and tossed it in the trash. Business was running as usual. Marcus loved his new business and he was blessed with dependable employees. There was no need for him to hang around. *I'm going home.*

As Marcus turned onto Chateau Estates, his heart rate began to increase. He felt an unexplainable disturbance in his soul and a strange connection in his conscious. He noticed Cashmere's SUV parked outside her home with the rear door open and the keys still lodged in the keyhole of her front door. The scene appeared odd to Marcus, but he kept driving as it was apparent that Cashmere did not want to be bothered with him. She was unaware that Marcus had purchased a home near her several months earlier. Marcus was beginning to feel invisible to Cashmere.

"I cannot be discouraged. My faith is stronger than this. Lord, give me the faith of Stephen and fill me with your Holy Ghost," Marcus prayed, as he lifted his right hand toward heaven. "Watch over Cashmere, keep her safe and comfort her with your precious love." Marcus had recited this same prayer for Cashmere each night before bed for the last twenty-three years.

Marcus pulled into his three car garage at 1853 Chateau Estates and as usual, went to check his mail. He bumped into a neighbor, Mrs. Borders, walking her dog. She stopped at Marcus's mailbox to rest and put her hand on her back and frowned. Her face appeared flushed and she was out of breath.

"Well, hello. How are you today, baby?" Mrs. Borders always called him that. She was in her late fifties, so it did not matter. She called everybody baby and always wore a white knit bonnet and a pink and white paisley dress.

"I'm fine, Mrs. Borders and yourself?" Marcus said, flipping through his mail.

"Oh, I'm just stretching these ole bones and walking my dog," she said adjusting her knee highs.

Marcus decided to make small talk with the lady in hopes of getting a glimpse of Cashmere when she returned to her truck. After about ten minutes of talking and glancing in the direction of Cashmere's house, Marcus asked Mrs. Borders if she knew how long the door had been opened on the black SUV parked up the street. Mrs. Borders told him it had been like that for quite some time, at least an hour. She suggested that Marcus investigate the situation to make sure everything was okay.

Sweat began to form on Marcus's head as worry set in. Without hesitation, he walked toward Cashmere's house, leaving Mrs. Borders and her dog behind. His walk turned into a jog which turned into a sprint. Marcus approached the Escalade and discovered that the hood was cold. He noticed Cashmere's purse still in the car and the keys still in the front door which was slightly ajar. Running up the steps, Marcus pushed the door open and found Cashmere on the floor.

"Cashmere, can you hear me?" Marcus pleaded as he hovered over her limp body. Afraid to move her, he called 911, gave them all of the information they needed, and then immediately returned to her side. "Cash, please talk to me. Can you hear me? Talk to me please. Oh, God, please help me."

Marcus felt desperate. He wrapped his arms around Cashmere while lying at her side; he wished he could fix whatever ailed her and make it all better. He looked around the room for a blanket and noticed the card he sent with her roses weeks ago. The roses had wilted and dried but they remained in a vase on her coffee table. Marcus reached in his wallet and pulled out a picture; a photograph so sacred to his heart that only God alone knew his thoughts. Overwhelmed with his feelings, he began to recite The Lord's Prayer and the 23rd Psalm. He was still gazing at the picture when the paramedics arrived.

Chapter 8

Olivia strutted into Lenox Mall early Saturday morning and went directly to her favorite store, Crate & Barrel. She was shopping for a variety of candles and home décor when she heard an announcement that took her attention away from the green crackled glass pitcher she had been eyeing.

"Thank you, ladies and gentlemen, for coming out today to show your support for V-103's annual talent show. We have recording agencies here today ready to sign a new record deal. All new registrants and participants line up in row #1 to speak with Larry Tinsley and all pre-registered auditioners should line up in row #2 to speak with Ryan Cameron. If you are under the age of eighteen, please see Mrs. Wanda Smith at the V-103 booth."

It was the voice of Frank Ski and Olivia pinched herself just to make sure she was not dreaming. Her heart felt as though it were threatening to stop its rhythm. She put one hand over her mouth and the other hand over her chest. "Could this be my chance? The opportunity I've waited for for a lifetime? All I want to do is sing. God you gave me this voice and I'm about to rock this house in the mighty, holy name of Jesus," she almost shouted as she moved toward row #1.

"Can I have your name please?" asked Larry Tinsley, sporting a V-103 hat with a matching t-shirt and a Colgate smile.

"Yes, it's Olivia Hamilton," she said smiling.

"Okay, just complete this information card and you're talent #29."

"Thank you so much," she said as she skirted away to quietly talk to God.

"Lord I need you to come through for me right now. I'm asking in Jesus' name that you will let me sing like never before. There are recording agencies here, Lord, ready to offer a record deal. Bless me Lord, and let the judges find favor within me. Give me the strength to praise and worship your name like never before. I bless your name Father and I claim the victory right now in Jesus' name. Let your light from heaven shine upon me. Fill this place with your holy anointing. Lord, I love you today and I worship your name. Thank you Jesus for this opportunity to minister to your people through song; in Jesus' name I pray. Amen."

"Talent #29, we will hear from you at this time," Frank Ski announced. "Please make your way to the stage area, talent #29."

The hour of waiting time that passed felt like a lifetime, but when Olivia finally heard her number called, she felt an anointing run all through her body. She felt God's hand resting on her shoulder. She knew without a shadow of a doubt that God had heard her prayer request. As she walked onto the stage, she received the microphone and immediately began to give God glory. Olivia reached way down deep within her soul and sang like an angel.

"Be blessed, don't live life in distress, just let go and let God work it out for you…"

When Olivia finished, she knew by the look on the audience members' faces that she had nailed it and for that, she gave God all the glory. The size of the crowd had doubled and she overheard people actually saying that she could be the next

Yolanda Adams. But Olivia did not want to be the next Yolanda; she only wanted what God had for her. The crowd went wild, giving her a standing ovation and chants of "Encore, Encore," echoed in the audience. It was a perfect performance and she knew it. As she walked off the stage a little girl with bright beaming eyes ran up to her and patted her on the thigh.

"Where did you learn to sing like that?" she asked, looking up at Olivia.

"I've been singing in the church choir since I was old enough to talk. My mother always took me with her to choir practice so I guess somewhere along the line, singing just came naturally."

"You are awesome."

"Thanks. But God is the awesome one. He gave me this talent and I just want to sing for Him." Olivia studied the little girl's face, imaging if anyone had ever told her about God. She wondered if the child had ever attended church or even knew any Christian hymns.

"You should…"

An announcement interrupted the girl's sentence. As a matter of fact, the entire area became quiet. The silence was almost deafening as everyone had their eyes glued on Frank Ski.

"It will take a while to tally all the judges' votes. We want to make sure we have an accurate count. Also we have two recording agencies here today. One of you lucky winners will walk away with a recording contract. Good luck to you all. Please feel free to shop or have lunch. The results will be announced in one hour."

With the announcement ended, the little girl spoke again. "You should be on TV," she said jumping up and down. "Have you ever watched Apollo?"

Olivia never had the chance to answer before the little girl's mother called for her, prompting the child to back away.

"Bye-bye," the girl yelled over her shoulder and waved. "I hope you win."

Olivia smiled inside as she witnessed the enthusiasm from her new little fan. Finally left to herself, she tried to call Melanie but there wasn't an answer. When she dialed Cashmere's telephone number, she got her voicemail. *Now where could those two hens be,* she mused silently. She was so overjoyed she could barely contain herself. The announcement regarding the record deal created a fire inside her soul. She believed God had placed her at Lenox Mall for a divine purpose. She knew it wasn't an accident or by luck but it was God directing her footsteps. As she walked to the food court, Olivia talked inwardly to her Heavenly Father.

Dear God you said in your Word in Matthew 7:7, Ask, and it shall be given you; seek, and ye shall find; knock, and it shall be opened unto you: For every one that asketh receiveth; and he that seeketh findeth; and to him that knocketh it shall be opened. Here I am God. I want to sing your praises and bless broken spirits with my voice. I want to use the talent that you gave me as a ministry to draw lost souls, heal the broken hearted, break and destroy yokes and most of all Lord, I want to sing praises unto your most holy and righteous name. Thank you Jesus for hearing my prayer and I claim it done right now in Jesus' name. I receive it Lord and I bless your name. Thank you for opening up the windows of heaven and pouring out this blessing upon me. I believe, Lord God, in my heart that this is my season and I give you all of the honor and the glory, forever. Amen.

Olivia was standing in line to buy Chinese food when a strange man walked up to her. He appeared homeless and weak, his clothes were filthy and he bore an offensive odor. His hair was mangled and unkempt, appearing to have not been cut in months. Worse yet, he was not wearing any shoes or socks.

"Excuse me, Miss," he groaned. "Could you spare some change? I am exhausted and so hungry."

That was believable. It seemed as though the young man had not eaten in days. He was merely a walking skeleton. Olivia's heart sank and she almost shook at the sight of this poor young man. He looked so torn and broken. Olivia began to search her purse for money but had none to give.

She looked into his weary eyes and said, "Sir, I apologize but I only have my debit card. I don't carry cash very often but I would be happy to buy you something to eat."

He nodded eagerly. "Thank you so much, Miss, I really appreciate this so much."

"Can I take your order?" the teenaged cashier asked Olivia as she and the ragged gentleman approached the counter.

"Yes, let me have two orders of Mongolian beef with fried rice and two egg rolls. To drink, we will have one large cup of sweet tea and a large cup of water."

"Sure, your total is $14.59."

Olivia swiped her debit card and entered her PIN number in the key pad. The young cashier gave her a receipt and thanked her for her order. When the food was ready, the young man extended his hand and offered to carry the tray to the table and Olivia allowed him to do so. Even though he looked like filthy rags, he was still a man. As they walked to the table, she began to remember several of her mother's favorite Bible verses in the book of James.

Chapter 2:2-3 says, For if there come unto your assembly a man with a gold ring, in goodly apparel, and there come in also a poor man in vile raiment; And ye have respect to him that weareth the gay clothing, and say unto him, Sit thou here in a good place; and say to the poor, Stand thou there, or sit here under my footstool:

Chapter 2:14-16 says, What doth it profit, my brethren, though a man say he hath faith, and have not works? If a brother or sister be naked, and destitute of daily food, and you say unto them, Depart in peace, be ye warmed and filled; notwithstanding ye give them not those things which are needful to the body; what doth it profit?

Remembrance of the scriptures reassured Olivia that she had made the right decision. She wanted to do everything pleasing in the eyesight of God.

"Is this table okay with you?" the man asked.

"Yes," she responded. "Wherever you choose to sit is fine with me, Mr....?"

"Oh, I'm so sorry. Forgive my manners; I'm just so tired. My name is Isaac. Isaac Davenport and you are?"

"My name is Olivia." She was about to sit down when Isaac excused himself from the table, stating that he did not want to intrude on her lunch. Deidre was not ashamed of his appearance nor did she mind the company so she told him he was welcome to join her. She even asked him to bless the food. Isaac seemed quite surprised. It was apparent that no one had ever been so kind to him before.

"So, tell me about yourself," Olivia inquired as they began eating.

"Well, I'm thirty-three years old and I was born in Louisiana and spent most of my childhood in an orphanage. When I finished high school, I enrolled in Job Corp in Morganfield, Kentucky where I got a degree in drafting."

"Growing up in an orphanage must have been tough," she assumed.

"It was horrible to say the least," Isaac replied.

"What brought you to Georgia?" Olivia asked as she took a sip of her water.

"I fell in love with a girl name Wynette. She had a close-knit loving family and when we graduated her family sort of adopted me as a part of them. I knew we could start a life together in Georgia. She was the love of my life. Her family became the family I never had. We were married shortly afterward and I landed a job as an architect with Osborn Construction in Atlanta," Isaac managed to say in between chews.

"That's my friend's father's company!" Olivia squealed with anticipation in her eyes.

"So then you know he expanded his business and moved to Waikiki."

"Right, that's correct. Is there a reason you decided not to go?" Olivia asked with a puzzled look on her face.

"Actually, I was offered a higher salary to relocate but Wynette refused to leave. Her father had just passed away two weeks prior and she did not want to leave her mother. I told Mr. Osborn that I would not be able to accept his offer to relocate. I loved my wife and her family dearly."

Olivia continued to talk with Isaac and listened as he shared a lot of personal information with her. He told her that he was not able to find another job to compete with his previous salary. Because of it, bills became delinquent and his and Wynette's home went into foreclosure. He began drinking alcohol and smoking marijuana to escape from the stress in his marriage. To soothe the ache in his heart and erase the memory of the pain in his wife's face, he turned to methamphetamines, which left him homeless and disconnected from everything and everyone he ever loved. Wynette could not stand to see her husband in such confusion. She tried to offer him counseling but he refused. After losing all they had and the man she loved, she eventually filed for divorce.

"Isaac do you still love your wife?" Olivia asked with tears welling in her eyes.

"More than life itself," Isaac confirmed with trembling lips trying to hide his emotions.

Olivia wondered what she could do to help Isaac. She had never been in a situation like this before but she knew she had been ordained by God to help him and she wanted to be obedient to the voice of the Lord.

With words of comfort and loving-kindness, she reached out to hold his hand. "Isaac, I want to help you."

He shook his head no. "You have done enough."

"Isaac you have touched my heart with your story. I can't walk away and not help you. Please let me help you." Immediately, Olivia lifted her hand toward heaven, praying, "Dear God, please bless Isaac. Forgive him of his sins and make him whole again. Renew in him a clean heart. Cleanse his body Lord, strengthen him and make him whole. Wash him in the precious blood of Jesus. Build him up where he's torn down. Fill every vein with your holy anointing. Break every demonic yoke in his body, mind and soul. Purify his soul, Lord; give him strength to be the man you called him to be. Change his appetite for drugs and alcohol. Free his mind, Lord, in the mighty name of Jesus. We declare it done and we give you all the thanks and the glory. Amen."

"Amen," cried Isaac. "Amen." Tears rolled heavily down his cheeks as he rejoiced in the presence of God. He had been touched and he knew it. People were walking by staring, but he did not notice them. He praised God like never before. Kids were pointing, but he did not care. He had waited so long for a miracle, a true breakthrough and he did not want to miss his opportunity for God to restore his life. Isaac slipped from his chair and fell down on his knees and began to cry out and travail in Jesus' name. He pleaded with God extensively to restore him and break all matter of evil off his life. He cried out for Jesus to save his soul and he repented for hurting Wynette. There were several people who came out of nowhere to circle around him and pray out loud in different tongues and languages. There was an anointing in the air so strong that people were being saved and slain in the Holy Spirit. Dozens were praying and asking for forgiveness and crying out for God to save their dying lost souls. God showed up and displayed His mighty power. It was an awesome experience and a life-changing event.

"Come with me," Olivia said, as she reached out for Isaac's hand. "I have a surprise for you," she said, smiling as they walked through the crowd and toward the exit sign. Olivia had been so caught up in the anointing and power of Jesus that she did not hear her name being announced as the winner of V-103's annual talent show and the receiver of a million dollar record contract.

Chapter 9

Marcus rode in the ambulance with Cashmere to Crawford Long Medical Center. It had been the longest ride of his life. The thought of her lying there helpless pierced a hole inside his heart. He held her hand and spoke to God until the paramedics rolled her into the emergency room.

Walking up to a nurse who stood behind the counter wearing a uniform bearing the nametag "Barbara," Marcus extended his hand that held Cashmere's purse. "This belongs to Cashmere, the patient that was just brought in. You may be able to find an insurance card or any other information you may need."

"Thank you sir, I will be taking care of everything. Our waiting area is around the corner."

Marcus sat in a corner seat adjacent to a window. It was a peaceful day, almost serene. There was not a cloud in the sky. From the place where he sat, Marcus could see birds flying in a single file line as if they were following instructions. He thought to himself how disciplined animals were and how their instincts were so incredible. He remembered as a child, how he would sit in his favorite tire swing, looking up at the birds wishing he could fly beside them in the clear blue sky. Marcus had a lonely childhood. Growing up in fos...

"If you need anything while your waiting, our cafeteria and snack bar is on the ground floor." Barbara explained, breaking Marcus's train of thought as she tapped him on the shoulder and then occupied the empty seat beside him.

Barbara had been the nurse assigned to Cashmere. Marcus also found out that she was an ordained pastor, called by God to share His message to lost and dying souls. Barbara always prayed for her patients, calling them by name. It was not a coincidence that Cashmere was assigned to Barbara. God always supplied the needs of His people.

"I entered all her information into the computer system. We are waiting on the report from Dr. Turner and as soon as we hear something we will let you know. I called someone by the name of Melanie, who was listed in her calendar book as her primary emergency contact, to let her know Cashmere was in the hospital. You can hold on to her purse for now..." Barbara's voice faded as she looked down to check her pager.

Marcus nodded. "She will be okay... this is just..."

"Barbara Henderson, please report to the ER, Barbara please report to the ER," an announcement blared over the intercom. Barbara stood up and immediately left to answer the call of duty. Marcus's heart sank as a lone tear streamed down his face.

Hours passed before he heard a word regarding Cashmere's condition. During the painfully slow waiting process, Marcus paced the floor and ate all of the mints out of the vending machine in an attempt to calm his nerves. Just as he was about to go find coffee, a lady walked his way and introduced herself as Melanie, Cashmere's friend.

The receptionist directed me your way and when I spotted you, I saw you with Cashmere's purse. I assume you are Cash's..." Melanie said doubtingly, waiting on Marcus to complete her sentence.

"I'm Marcus," he said while trying to pull his thoughts together.

"Oh…so *you* are Marcus," Melanie said with a sly grin that turned serious again. "So, what happened and what's going on?"

"I was on my way home when I noticed her keys in the front door of her house and the door of her vehicle left open. After talking to one of my neighbors, I discovered that Cash's SUV's rear door and house door had been left opened for over an hour and a half so I went to check on her and found her lying unconscious on the living room floor."

Melanie's voice rose. "What? Oh no, will she be okay? Has anyone called her parents in Hawaii? Oh, my… I have to…"

"You have to claim down so you can think," Marcus said. "You are her friend and you need to talk to the doctors. They aren't going to give me much information, but they will talk to you. You'll have to be Cash's mouthpiece until she regains consciousness."

"She still hasn't regained consciousness?" Melanie cried, raising her hands up and down. Her cries began to get louder as she fell into Marcus's arms. Something about him was familiar, but Melanie was too upset to recognize the resemblance.

Barbara returned and rushed by Melanie's side, wrapping her arms around her in comfort. "Is everything okay?"

"I'm Melanie. You're the nurse that called me here," Melanie said after spotting the nametag on her uniform. "I'm so worried about my friend; please tell me how she's doing?"

"She's still groggy, but we have run several tests and her vital signs have been stabilized and her blood pressure is back to normal. We have her on an IV for pain. She has regained consciousness, and that was our greatest concern. You can see her after we transport her to a regular room. She's going to be okay." Barbara patted Melanie on the shoulder as she spoke.

"Thank goodness," Melanie exhaled, regaining her composure while searching through her purse for an aspirin. With all this nervous tension, she needed a pain reliever of her own.

This was the best news Marcus had heard all day. He was ecstatic. "Thank you Jesus," he shouted. "Thank you so much."

Melanie wondered what in the world he was so thankful for. *He doesn't know her from Adam or Eve.*

"Would you like to join me for coffee in the cafeteria?" Marcus asked Melanie.

"Sure, I need to make a few phone calls and I'll be right there."

"Has she been sick or complaining about her health?" Marcus inquired when he and Melanie were finally sharing a table.

"She has been complaining about stomach pains and very bad cramps in her lower abdominal area. But that's it," Melanie recalled.

"That's enough to see a doctor, don't you think?" Marcus frowned, staring at Melanie with a confused look in his eyes. "Did you suggest she see a doctor?"

"Yes, but Cash is stubborn; and she doesn't like the sight of hospitals or the doctor's office."

"How long have you two been friends?"

"Since third grade."

"Really?" Marcus questioned, leaning back in his chair.

"Yes, we have been friends for a very long time."

"Tell me about her," Marcus said with a grin.

"Why do you want to know about Cash? Are you two dating?"

"No, not yet."

"You sure are confident. If the roses did not make her go out with you, what can?" Melanie stood up and walked away to get more cream for her coffee.

"I'm a nice guy, Melanie." Marcus stood up when Melanie excused herself from the table. He was taught to always stand as a show of respect whenever a woman excused herself from the table.

Melanie turned around and noticed Marcus still standing and almost dropped her creamer. This gesture caught her off guard. Richmond had been the only man she'd known to be a true gentleman of that caliber. "All men are nice in the beginning," she scolded, sounding cynical as she returned to her seat.

Marcus walked behind her chair to scoot it forward for her as she sat. "I'm not all men, I'm Marcus and I'm different."

Melanie was completely taken aback at Marcus's kind mannerism. She found it delightful to be in the presence of a well-mannered man. She felt very comfortable with Marcus but she needed to find out more information so she could advise Cashmere.

"So, tell me about yourself, Mr. Marcus."

Taking his seat, Marcus stirred his coffee. "I'm a very respectful man. I love God and I am a very sincere Christian. My favorite thing to do is cook and I love gospel music."

"Sounds interesting," Melanie said. "Any kids?"

"No kids, although someday I plan to have a big family. I love children," Marcus said, smiling thinking of all the kids he grew up with.

"Wives, ex-wives or girlfriends?" Melanie asked.

"I have neither," replied Marcus, with raised eyebrows.

"Good," said Melanie." You might be a keeper."

Marcus looked at Melanie with a fashionable smile. "I'm more than a keeper. I am more than a conqueror through Jesus Christ who loves and strengthens me."

"What? You quote scriptures too? I can't wait to tell Cash this," Melanie snickered, shaking her head back and forth.

When Marcus laughed, something about the jovial outburst sounded oddly familiar to Melanie. She felt as though she had known him all her life. He had a face she almost recognized and a wholesome spirit that felt relatable.

"I'm going to ask her to marry me," Marcus announced proudly, rubbing his hands together as he spoke.

"What...?" Melanie asked in shock, spitting coffee from her mouth. "Are you crazy? Cash is not going to marry you, she doesn't even know you."

"She will be my wife; it's already been predestined."

"You had me going along with you at first, but now I'm beginning to think you are on the coo-coo side," Melanie said, her face showing no signs of humor. "Is something wrong with you Marcus?"

He stared at her for awhile without saying a word. This worried Melanie. She had no idea what he was thinking. For all she knew, Marcus was a psychopath.

"Look Marcus, it was nice meeting you. I'm sure you are a nice person," Melanie said cautiously while readying to leave the table.

Without saying a word to prelude his actions, Marcus reached out and gently grabbed her arm, motioning for Melanie to have a seat. When he had her undivided attention, Marcus pulled a picture from his wallet. He had been carrying the picture around for years. It was a hand drawn image of a woman whose face was identical to Cashmere's. Marcus gazed at the picture for a while before he began to speak. Tears welled heavily in his eyes and plunged down his face like a river fall. He finally made eye contact with Melanie and then handed her the picture.

"I grew up in foster care. I didn't have much to believe in until one day, I went to the fair as a part of a class fieldtrip. I was only thirteen years old. There was a lady at the fair who looked to be in her late fifties and she had a booth set up and was prophesying. I walked by and she called out my name. She introduced herself as Margie Alberta and she took my hand and instantly started to draw a sketch of my future wife which is this very picture that you hold in your hands now. Margie told me that God had ordained me to love her with an agape love. I had been chosen to mend her broken heart, to cater to her every emotional desire, to fulfill her greatest fantasy, to cherish her like a precious jewel and to honor her all the days of my life. She told me not to look for her but that one day I would find her when the time was right. Margie instructed me to carry this picture in my wallet. She told me her name would be Cashmere and I would find her when she needed me the most."

Tears were flowing down Melanie's face too. No one knew better than Melanie how Cashmere deserved a man to love her unconditionally. Her heart had been used, abused and neglected. She gave all and got nothing in return. She fulfilled only to be left empty. She stayed when she should have left. Cashmere had a heart pure as gold but gave it to the wrong man.

"I have saved myself for Cashmere; I have been waiting on her all my life," Marcus said quietly. His eyes were closed as though he was reliving the entire childhood episode in his mind.

"You've never had a girlfriend, Marcus?" Melanie scowled, causing wrinkles to her forehead.

"I've never had a girlfriend," Marcus admitted. A brief half-smile showed on his face when he added, "I've never even been kissed by a woman and I'm thirty six years old."

"Marcus...are you saying you are a ..." Melanie stopped in mid-sentence.

"A virgin. Yes, I am very proud to say I am a virgin. I've waited for Cashmere all my life and I am ready to give myself to her as God's most precious gift."

Chapter 10

"**H**oney, honey…where are you?" cried Mrs. Osborn. "Honey, we have to fly to Georgia, something is wrong with Cash, she's in the hospital."

"Oh, Jesus, please watch over my baby girl," Mr. Osborn pleaded. "Let's go to the airport, we don't have time to pack."

With her husband's coaching, Mrs. Osborn calmed herself enough to get through security lines without raising concerns among the airport staff. She knew she had to keep her emotions in check if they were to clear the heightened security. If her behavior was erratic, they would never be allowed on board and she would never get to Cashmere in a timely manner.

"We just saw her and she seemed fine. I hope everything is okay. She's our only child. What if something terrible has happened?" Mrs. Osborn's hysteria began to return once she and her husband had settled in their seats and the plane took flight.

"Baby, you have to calm down," Mr. Osborn reminded her. "Cash is in the Lord's hands. She's going to be alright. You must believe that." When his wife's tears continued to flow, he tried again, whispering in her ear and holding her close to him. "Baby, please stop crying, you're going to make yourself sick. You have to be strong for Cash; now I need you to pull yourself together."

"Can I get you anything?" a young stewardess asked with concern in her eyes.

Mr. Osborn flashed a brief appreciative smile and said, "Yes, please bring her a coke."

"Would you like anything, sir?"

"No, not at the moment, but thanks." Mr. Osborn knew that he had to be strong for his wife and for Cashmere. His heart was bleeding on the inside. He knew Cashmere had just recently gotten out of a terrible relationship; one that they did not approve of from the beginning. He wanted his daughter to be treated like a queen and it hurt him to witness her stay in a mentally abusive relationship for nine years. Now that she had left Donovan, she had made him the happiest father alive.

Looking out the window, he remembered when Cashmere was thirteen and in the hospital. She had fallen at cheerleading practice and as a result, she suffered temporary amnesia. Back then, Mr. Osborn was worried sick, but nothing compared to how he felt at this very moment. He was hours and miles away from his baby girl.

Closing his eyes to concentrate on God, he prayed, whispering just loud enough for his wife to hear. "Dear God, please stretch forth your hand to Cash. Lord fix whatever is ailing her body. Go into the hospital room and comfort her with your Spirit. Touch her body from her head to her feet. Be with her, Jesus; keep her in the bosom of Abraham. Lord, you gave this child to us and I ask that you restore her body one hundred fold. Make her brand new. Wash her body in your precious blood. Build her mind, body and soul. Give her a clean heart. I ask this prayer in Jesus' name. Amen."

"Amen," whispered Mrs. Osborn. Moments later, just after finishing the last of the soda that had been brought to her, she relaxed against her husband's shoulder and drifted to sleep.

It was early Sunday morning when The Osborns arrived in Atlanta. As they walked through the terminal at Hartsfield-Jackson Airport, they felt relieved to be one step closer to

Cashmere. Mr. Osborn managed to find a taxi to take them to Crawford Long Medical Center. The taxi was very clean and the driver seemed extremely nice and eager to help.

"I'll take you there right away," The cab driver said, with a Jamaican accent. "Do you have family in the hospital?"

"Yes, our daughter," Mr. and Mrs. Osborn responded softly as they continued looking out of the window. They both were reminiscing over all the good times they had while living in Georgia. Mr. Osborn sat silently, remembering the first building he built while Mrs. Osborn thought of all her friends and family. Hawaii had welcomed them with open arms and allowed them the opportunity to expand their business, but there was nothing like being home.

As the cab driver maneuvered his car into a space near the hospital entrance, a knot tied in Mrs. Osborn's stomach. She was nervous and did not know exactly what to expect.

"Here we are; you folks have a nice day," the driver announced, looking over his shoulder.

"You do the same. How much is the fare?" Mr. Osborn asked.

"No charge, my man, just go check on your daughter. I pray she's well."

"No, I can't let you do that. I have to pay you," Mr. Osborn stated.

"I'm positive sir; the fare is on me today. Now go, I insist... your daughter needs you."

Mrs. Osborn was already inside speaking with the receptionist by the time her husband joined her.

"She's in room three eighty-eight," the receptionist said while looking at the computer screen, not noticing that Mrs. Osborn had already dashed down the hall.

"Thank you," Mr. Osborn said to the receptionist just before turning away to catch up with his wife. She was already on the elevator calling for him to hurry.

"Come on, honey," she called, holding the door open for him.

"I'm moving as fast as my legs will carry me." Mr. Osborn almost had to run to catch up and was nearly out of breath as he spoke. The elevator was crowded with people displaying an array of emotions. Some were crying, a few were laughing, but most were quiet. For Mr. Osborn who hated being crowded in closed quarters, the ride to the third floor was uncomfortable.

When they arrived at room three eighty-eight, they looked at each other and inhaled deeply. Awakened by the opening of the door, Cashmere opened her eyes.

"Mama, Daddy..." With weak arms, Cashmere tried to reach out to them. Tears flowed down her face but her heart was full of joy. She loved her parents more than words would ever say.

"Daddy," Cashmere cried as she looked up at him, "I am so happy you are here. Please take me home. I want to go home."

"Cash, honey, you are sick and you need to stay in the hospital. We took the first flight in that we could catch and we haven't had a chance to talk to the doctor yet."

Mrs. Osborn reached out and rubbed her daughter's head with tender soft strokes. "How are you feeling Cashmere?" she asked with concern in her voice.

"I feel okay; the pain medication is starting to work."

"I'm going to talk with the nurse, I'll be right back." Mrs. Osborn turned to walk away. Halfway up the hall, she met Melanie and a gentlemen walking toward Cashmere's room.

"Mrs. Osborn, hi, how is she?" Melanie inquired.

"Well, I really don't know much, I'm on my way to find her doctor so he can tell me what's going on with my child."

"Before you go, Mrs. Osborn, this is Marcus, he found Cash unconscious on her living room floor and called 911," Melanie explained.

"Unconscious?" Mrs. Osborn frowned. "Why would Cash pass out?"

"For over a month, she had been complaining of stomach cramps and pain in her lower abdomen. I suggested she see a doctor but you know how Cash feels about hospitals and doctors' offices," Melanie said, trying to be informative as possible.

Marcus extended his hand to Mrs. Osborn. "Hello, I'm Marcus; it's nice to finally meet you."

Melanie gave him a nudge in his side as a signal for him to stop speaking. She did not want Marcus to give Mrs. Osborn a heart attack with the news of proposing marriage to her daughter. Although Mrs. Osborn was surprised by his use of the word "finally," she pushed the inquiry out of her mind as she noticed a doctor walking in their direction. He had a chart in his hand looking over information that had been written there.

"Excuse me, would you happen to have any information on Cashmere Osborn?" Mrs. Osborn inquired.

"Sure, she's my new patient and I'm on my way to see her," Dr. Turner responded.

"I'm her mother, please tell me about her condition," pleaded Mrs. Osborn.

"Certainly, ma'am. Follow me into the patient family conference room, please."

Mrs. Osborn's body tightened with every step she took while following the doctor's lead. She braced herself for the information regarding Cashmere, hoping and praying inwardly that God would prepare her for whatever she was about to hear. Melanie and Marcus followed and she was thankful that she wouldn't hear the news alone. Inside the conference room, all eyes were focused on Dr. Turner.

"Cashmere suffers from anemia, which means that her number of red blood cells is lower than it should be. The results of one of the exams we performed also shows that her uterus is enlarged. This inflammation is caused by two fibroid tumors in the walls of her uterus. In this particular situation, we normally would perform a hysterectomy, but Cashmere does not have any children and to keep from taking that option away from her, we would like to discuss two other alternatives to the radical surgery," he said closing the file and placing it on his lap.

The room was silent momentarily. Everyone was either in shock or prayerful meditation. Dr. Turner leaned forward and placed a hand on Mrs. Osborn's shoulder. He knew the pain she was feeling. It was written all over her face.

"If you'll excuse me, I need to talk to Cashmere to discuss the options with her first. She has important decisions to make," he sighed as he turned to walk away. Once outside of the listening range of Cashmere's visitors, Dr. Turner began mumbling to himself as he walked down the long hospital hall. "This will not be easy. In all my years of practice, I still find it hard to break such disappointing news; especially to a woman that has not birthed any children."

Chapter 11

Olivia walked into her kitchen to prepare her first meal of the morning. She decided to cook pancakes, turkey bacon and cheese eggs. As she reached into the refrigerator to gather her items, her cell phone rang. Olivia didn't recognize the number on the caller ID, but answered the line anyway.

"Hello?"

"Hello, may I speak with Olivia Hamilton, please?" a strange chipper voice said from the other end.

"This is Olivia," she replied, leaning against her refrigerator.

"Olivia, my name is Velincia and I have very exciting news for you. You entered a talent show a couple of days ago at Lenox Mall and you have been chosen as the winner of the V-103 talent show as well as the recipient of a one million dollar contract with Gospo Centric Productions."

"Stop playing," Olivia said, still holding the breath she'd taken in when the caller started her second sentence.

"It's true, you are the winner." Velincia assured her. "You stole the judges' hearts. It's been a long time since we've heard that type of talent. Congratulations."

Olivia screamed so loud she could have awakened the dead. She jumped up and down in excitement and her body trembled as she could not contain her emotions. Tears of joy rolled down her face and a smile rose in Olivia's heart. She dropped the phone and fell to her knees, thanking God for answering her prayer. She had been so caught up in Isaac's miracle deliverance in the food court at the mall that day that she had forgotten about the talent show.

Olivia looked up, lifted her hands toward heaven and began to praise and worship God wholeheartedly. "God you said in your Word that if I only have the faith of a mustard seed that I could move mountains. My faith and trust I put in thee and you answered my cry. Thank you, Lord for looking down and blessing me. I praise your most holy name. I love you, Jesus. You are my redeemer. Oh, Lord…thank you, Jesus. I lift your name on high. I praise you, I lift you up, and I magnify your name. Lord, you are worthy to be praised. Guide my footsteps; let my light shine so others will see your glorious works. Send a multitude of angels to guide my path. Let my music minister to lost souls so that your people will be freed from Satan's vicious hold. I thank you right now in Jesus' name. Amen. Amen. Amen."

Olivia's praise evolved into a cheerful beam as she realized the number of lives she could touch with her angelic voice. She contemplated the enormous responsibility but instantly felt peace in her soul. Picking the phone back up and realizing that Velincia was still on the other end of the line, Olivia apologized for the temporary abandonment and then added, "Velincia, I'm so thankful. I am so full of the Spirit I can hardly contain myself. I have waited on this moment all my life. This is not a fantasy; this is real. My dream has come true."

"You deserve it and we look forward to working with you and watching your career blossom," Velincia stated. "We would like to meet with you on Wednesday morning to finalize all the important papers. Is ten o'clock good for you?"

"Ten o'clock is perfect."

"Okay, we'll see you Wednesday at ten," Velincia said, simultaneously penciling in Olivia's appointment.

CASHMERE CRIES

As Olivia ended the call and resumed her task of preparing her breakfast, she suddenly felt perturbed in her spirit. Just that quickly, her jubilation waned as concern set in. She wondered what Melanie was doing and why neither she nor Cashmere had returned her call. Picking up the phone she'd just hung up moments earlier, Olivia tried calling Melanie again but again, there was no answer. Pacing the floor, she felt something must be wrong. It was not like Melanie to not answer her telephone. Convincing herself that she was overacting, Olivia decided to give her a call again after she finished eating. Just as she was cracking her eggs in the skillet, her cell phone rang.

It was Melanie, and Olivia didn't want to waste any time sharing her good news. "Girl, I have something to tell you! I …"

Melanie abruptly interrupted her moment of triumph. "Okay, but first I have to tell you that Cash is in the hospital."

Olivia froze. Nothing moved on her body but her eyeballs, up and down and then side to side. A frown appeared on Olivia's face. The news of Cashmere being in the hospital did not seem realistic. "What hospital?" she asked after finding her voice.

"Crawford Long Medical Center; room three eighty-eight. I'll tell you more when you get here. Just meet me in the family patient conference room on the third floor."

Olivia and Melanie released the call simultaneously. Olivia believed in her heart that Cashmere would be okay but still, she sent up an earnest prayer before turning off her stove, abandoning the half-cooked meal, and driving to the hospital.

While in route, she called her assistant choir director. "Hey Erin, this is Olivia. I hate to call you on such short notice but I need you to direct the choir this morning. I am on my way to the hospital."

"Sure no problem, I hope everything is okay," Erin said.

Not wanting to divulge her friend's personal information, Olivia replied, "I hope so too," and then released the call.

For years, Olivia had directed all the choirs at her church. She would miss her duties in this morning's service, but today, God had a bigger calling for her life.

❋ ❋ ❋ ❋ ❋

Dr. Turner took a deep breath as he knocked on the door and entered Cashmere's room. He observed the man sitting on her bed who looked to be in his mid sixties. Dr. Turner immediately noticed how distinctive the man looked. He was dressed in fine navy slacks with a tan polo shirt. His salt and pepper curly hair formed sideburns along both sides of his face which also folded into a mustache and goatee. He looked at Cashmere and knew instantly where she received her good looks. He thought Mrs. Osborn, with her voluptuous curves and flawless sandy brown skin, was beautiful enough to make a blind man see. He had noticed that she had hair like an Egyptian queen and eyes that danced like magic. With such attractive parents, it was no wonder that Cashmere was such a striking young woman.

"Knock-knock..." Dr. Turner finally said after a brief stance in the room. "Hello, my name is Dr. Turner. I have your test results, Cashmere," he said walking closer to her bed. "How are you feeling?" he added as he reached out to hold her hand.

"Okay, I guess," Cashmere mumbled while rubbing her free hand across her face.

"You must be Dad. How are you today sir?" Dr. Turner asked Mr. Osborn.

He nodded and smiled. "I'm just fine."

Dr. Turner turned his attention again to his patient. "Cashmere you have a condition called anemia, which means your blood count is very low. It's not an uncommon condition, however, your hemoglobin, or red blood pigment, is lower than most. I have prescribed special iron tablets for you. I want you to begin taking three pills a day for seven days. Then two pills a day for seven days and then one pill a day from that point on. This will boost your blood count tremendously. It may cause constipation, but just remember to drink eight to ten glasses of water each day. Will you do that for me?" he asked.

"I will," she answered.

"Now let's move on to more serious concerns." Dr. Turner put on his glasses and pulled up a chair beside Cashmere's bed. "Miss Osborn, we found fibroid tumors in your uterus."

"You found what?" Cashmere asked with a look of confusion on her face as she tried to sit up in bed.

"Two fibroid tumors, approximately the size of small eggs, are in the walls of your uterus, one on each side. Fifty percent of African-American women develop these during their lifetime however, fibroids are usually not cancerous." Dr. Turner tried to sound comforting as he saw the increased tension in Cashmere's face.

"How did this happen to me? What treatment will I need? What caused this in my body? Daddy, I don't understand." Tears flooded down her face as she buried her head in her father's chest.

Mr. Osborn held her in his arms – so close she could hear his heartbeat. He felt helpless. He had always been able to protect his daughter but at this moment all the money in the world could not explain his baby's condition.

"So far, medical studies are not capable of explaining why a number of women develop uterine fibroids when others do not, I believe genetics play a major role. Treatment used to be limited to hysterectomy only," the doctor explained.

A hysterectomy? I don't even have any children yet. I can't possibly have a hysterectomy, Cashmere vexed silently.

"Since you do not have any children, I'd like to present you with two other options." Dr. Turner looked at her and thought how awful it would be to end reproduction within the Osborn generation. They were such a gorgeous family, not just outwardly attractive, but inwardly as well. He glanced at Mr. Osborn and saw the disappointment in his eyes at the possibility of not having grandchildren.

"What are my options?" Cashmere moaned, sniffling and rubbing her tears away as head remained nestled in her father's chest.

Dr. Turner crossed his legs as he leaned forward and sat on the edge of his chair. "You will either have to become pregnant soon or we can try a procedure called Uterine Artery Embolization."

Cashmere's sniffles turned into a louder cry as frustration emerged onto her face. "I cannot become pregnant now," she cried. "My divorce was final a month ago... I am single now." Cashmere felt her heart break into a million pieces. She was confused, weary and hurt. "How am I supposed to get married and pregnant so instantly?"

"I'll marry you." The unexpected deep sexy voice filled the room, startling everyone.

Cashmere looked up, trying to focus her exhausted eyes. "Marcus?"

He had heard Cashmere's cries and he walked into the room carrying forty-eight yellow long stemmed roses.

Mr. Osborn looked over his shoulder and immediately recognized Marcus. He moved out of the way, allowing Marcus to approach Cashmere's bedside. All eyes were on Marcus as he took Cashmere's hand and got down on one knee.

Chapter 12

Mr. Osborn and Dr. Turner quickly left room three eighty-eight. Cashmere's father rushed into the family patient waiting room leaving Dr. Turner behind. His smile was brighter than the sun. His heart was full of joy, unspeakable joy. He even hummed... "Oh...joy, joy...God's great joy."

Mr. Osborn dashed into the waiting room, nearly colliding with Olivia and Rich as they all were about to enter the doorway at the same time. Olivia wanted to speak with him but it was obvious that he was in a hurry. Mr. Osborn's skin was glowing and his eyes were big, as if he had seen a ghost. He waved to everyone and nodded quickly. His major concern was talking to Mrs. Osborn.

"Baby...come with me." Mr. Osborn reached out to help his wife out of the lounge chair.

Mrs. Osborn looked puzzled. "Honey, is everything okay with Cash?"

He nodded. "She's fine baby, just come with me please," he said as he ushered her out of the waiting area.

Mrs. Osborn's mind was traveling rapidly. She could not possibly imagine what in the world her husband was so excited about. He was moving so fast, she almost broke the heel on her shoe in her efforts to keep up. "Honey, please slow down. I haven't seen you move this fast in years."

As they approached the exit sign, Mrs. Osborn was completely out of breath. Mr. Osborn pushed the door open that led to the outside terrace. He inhaled deeply, and then reached for his wallet and pulled out a hand drawn picture. "Baby, do you remember when Cash was thirteen years old, how she fell at cheerleading practice and suffered temporally memory lost?"

She nodded. "Yes."

Panting, Mr. Osborn swallowed hard. "Well, a couple of days before her accident, I had taken her to the fair. We were walking along when a lady who appeared to be in her late fifties called out Cashmere's name. She had a booth set up and was prophesying. She took Cash's hand and instantly started to draw a picture of her future husband which is this very picture I hold in my hands. She told Cash that God had ordained this man to love her with an agape love. He had been chosen to mend her broken heart, to cater to her every emotional desire, to fulfill her greatest fantasy, to cherish her like a precious jewel and to honor her all the days of his life. She told Cash not to look for him but that one day, when the time was right, he would find her. The prophet instructed Cash to carry this picture in her purse. She told Cash his name would be Marcus and he would find her when she needed him the most."

Elated, he continued. "After Cash's accident she did not recall the events that happened at the fair. One day I was in her room, and I saw the picture in the trashcan so I picked it up and put it in my wallet. Being a father and a man of God, I prayed Marcus would eventually find Cash and treat her like a princess; just the way I have treated you all these years."

"Why are you telling me this now?"

"Baby, you were not yourself. You had just buried Mr. B. and things were just so crazy. Then with Cashmere's accident; it was just too much for you to bear. So, I just didn't mention it."

Looking up at her husband with an odd frown on her face, Mrs. Osborn asked, "Is that why you opposed her marriage to Donovan; because you believed what a lady said at the fair?"

"For the most part, yes; but, I never approved of Donovan anyway. He was not the man on this picture. He was not the image I had prayed for in my mind all those years. He was not Marcus. I tried to tell Cash to wait but before I knew anything, she had eloped." Mr. Osborn held his face in his hands at the painful recall.

"Honey, why are you telling me this now?" Mrs. Osborn asked again.

He looked at her with a smile on his face. "Baby, he's in her room and he just asked her to marry him!" Mr. Osborn was about to explode in excitement.

"Marcus? The same Marcus that was in the patient family waiting room with Melanie?" Mrs. Osborn finally realized that this was the same young man she had been talking to earlier. Now she understood what Marcus meant when he used the word "finally". She also remembered how he charged out of the room and whispered, "She needs me" to himself as he grabbed his chest. She looked up at her husband. His eyes caught her gaze and they stared at each other for quite some time without speaking. Mr. Osborn leaned over to embrace his wife, and then they walked hand in hand back to their daughter's room.

❊ ❊ ❊ ❊ ❊

In the waiting room, Melanie told Richmond and Olivia everything that had happened with Cashmere and Marcus. They had always known that Donovan was not the man for Cashmere, but that didn't lessen their shock. They hoped Marcus was truly God sent.

Richmond received a text message from Michael requesting that he return his call at his earliest convenience. His earlier conversation with Michael had been interrupted when Melanie called, asking him to come to the hospital. As Richmond walked across the room to use the phone in the waiting area, he noticed a sign on the wall that read *Three Minutes Only*; so instead, he walked into the lobby to use one of the payphones.

He took a deep breath as he dialed Michael's telephone number, hoping he would have some information to pull this puzzle together. "Hey, Michael, this is Richmond. Do you have any information?" Rich pulled up a chair to have a seat. Preparing himself for whatever information would be given, he reached into his pocket to pull out a pen and a small notepad.

"Man, I hope you are sitting down. I spoke to Mom earlier today and from the information she told me, apparently your birth mother's name is Sallie Ann Davenport. She was born in Vivian, Louisiana and she was a single mother who never married. However, she had a lifelong boyfriend by the name of William B. Wallis, who is your father. And get this; you also have two younger brothers who were fathered by the same man."

Richmond's mouth fell open. "You're kidding." Richmond stood up in excitement. "I do not believe what I'm hearing," he said, rubbing his hands on his bald head.

"Rich, you were adopted by Mr. and Mrs. Miccoli, correct?" Michael doubled checked.

"That's correct," Rich said, folding his arms while balancing the phone between the side of his head and his shoulder.

"Okay, one of your brothers was put in a foster home and the other in an orphanage. Mom could not quite remember their names but she thought it may be Marc...Mario...Malcolm, anyway, she says it's something of the sort. And the other name was something like, Isaiah...Ike...Irvin; she couldn't remember the exact names. But she promised when she found out their correct names, she would give me a call."

"Do you know why she gave us away?" Rich inquired, as his heart began a quick, heavy rhythm.

"Mom mentioned that Ms. Sallie had birthed three boys for Mr. Wallis who was a very wealthy man in town, not to mention he was the mayor and a deacon of New Hope Baptist Church. He did not want his wife to find out any information regarding his affair or his children, so each time Ms. Sallie became pregnant, he demanded she give away the babies after birth. Evidently, he did not want a town scandal involving his name."

Michael continued to talk, but Rich dropped the phone as he felt total pain all over his body. He backed away from the phone and watched as it dangled from side to side. The voice of Michael calling out his name drove him farther into his isolated thoughts. He walked in a daze for what seems like hours as he imagined his brothers growing up in an orphanage and foster home. He really didn't care if his parents were dead or alive; he just wanted to find his brothers. He could not believe a parent could have such shallow love for their children. Rich felt rage and sadness at the same time. No matter what type of parents he had, it was time for him and Melanie to make a family of their own.

Chapter 13

Cashmere stared into the sincere eyes that belonged to Marcus. She felt something inside her soul. Words could not describe the sensation that circled her body as he held her hand, still kneeling on one knee. She knew instantly in her heart that she could marry this man and live happily ever after. He just had a Godly presence that seemed to ooze out of his flesh. Cashmere had waited so long to be loved and respected unconditionally. She remembered how gentle and concerned Marcus had been with her and how safe and secure she felt in his arms. As Cashmere looked across the ensemble of roses that graced her bed and the 5.5 carat canary colored diamond ring, she only saw the love in his eyes. Her eyes connected with his and love captured her soul.

"Marcus, we barely even know each other," Cashmere said, looking away from him.

"Cash, I believe God knows best. He doesn't make mistakes," Marcus replied, using his hand to return her face toward his.

"But what about my condition?"

"Marry me," he whispered.

"But what about children?"

"Marry me," he said, kissing her hands.

"But..."

Marcus placed his finger over her lips. "Marry me," he pleaded, caressing her face softly. "I am in love with you. I have loved you for a very long time. I have prayed for you for years. I have kept my heart pure for your love only. My body is undefiled. I am a wholesome man. I can love you and you only until the end of time. Cash, this is right. God doesn't make mistakes. I feel you right here," he whispered, pointing to the place on his chest that was directly in front of his heart. "When you cry, I cry. When you're happy, so am I. When your heart beats, my heart beats. We are connected on a spiritual level that is so far beyond our understanding. Cashmere I love you, please say you'll be my wife."

She nodded. Cashmere could not control what she felt any longer. She could not hide the feelings that captured her heart and her entire being. For once, Cashmere felt complete. For once she felt true love. Her soul identified with his soul as the passion from his heart rolled off his tongue. She knew in her spirit it was right. Tears rolled down her face as she said, "Yes, I'll marry you, Marcus."

Marcus leaped to his feet and held her body as tightly against his as the hospital bed would allow. He lifted his hands toward heaven and began to worship God. He cried out thanking God as tears flowed down his face. "Lord, thank you for Cashmere. Thank you Lord for all that you have done for me in my life. I was obedient to your Word. I believe you can do all things. I believe you will heal Cashmere. I claim it done in Jesus' name. I trust you, Lord. Bring forth healing to her body just as you did for the woman who had the issue of blood. Fill her with love. Anoint her body from head to toe. Cleanse her body with the blood of the Lamb. Wash her, Lord, pure as snow. Prepare her womb to conceive, Lord. I ask that you bless my seed. I ask that you fill her womb with your Holy Spirit in Jesus' name. Amen."

Sounds of "Amen" overflowed in Cashmere's room. She and Marcus were so involved in praying, they did not notice the crowd that encircled them. Olivia was praying alongside Marcus as well as Cashmere's parents. Melanie tried praying, but couldn't. With a mounting desire for God's anointing in her life, all she could do was nod her head. Marcus's testimony had brought tears to Melanie's eyes. It made her realize that God was truly real. Melanie knew that Olivia and Cashmere were raised in Bible-believing homes. However Melanie's house was quite the opposite. Her parents were not atheists but they were not Spirit-filled either. Her best recollection of church was dressing up on Easter morning, in a pretty dress and carrying an Easter basket. Melanie stepped aside to witness the power of God and the flowing of His presence. She yearned for what they experienced and she knew in her heart it was time to make a change.

❊ ❊ ❊ ❊ ❊

On the ride home, Richmond shared with Melanie everything Michael had told him. The distraught look on his face caused her to worry about him. She had never seen her husband so distressed. She thought of many ways to comfort him but nothing helped. Melanie looked out the window and thought of how life can turn so drastically in a matter of seconds. She wanted to know God for herself. She wanted to have peace, joy and happiness in her soul. She needed and wanted to feel God's power unleashed in her life.

Once, inside their condo, Rich sat down at the kitchen table and cried like a newborn. He felt the world on his shoulders and for once in life, he felt like a failure. He sobbed uncontrollably at the reminder of being born an unwanted child. He thought to himself that he was a helpless infant; he did not ask to be brought into the world. He felt rage as he thought of how his father used his birth mother for his sick fleshly pleasure.

Melanie held her husband throughout the night as he wept. Richmond's body was so feeble from crying that he didn't even seem to have the strength to make it to the bedroom. Instead he crumpled his body onto the kitchen floor, sleeping the night on the hard uncomfortable surface, with his wife beside him.

Chapter 14

Richmond groaned as he tried to awaken from a deep sleep. His body soon realized that he was not in his king size bed. Rubbing his eyes, he sat up as the sun began to peep through the bay window. As he stood, he saw a note, written in large letters, adhered to the refrigerator's door.

> *Richmond, you were sleeping like a baby. I did not want to disturb you. I hope you feel better today. Just know that I love you and together we will get through this. I am going to the hospital. Cash is being discharged at eleven o'clock.*
>
> *All my love,*
> *Melanie*

He sat down at the table with a box of his favorite Captain Crunch cereal. As a child, Richmond remembered eating his cereal while watching the Smurfs, a once popular cartoon, on Saturday mornings. He loved watching the blue characters use their intelligence to protect their village.

Richmond had always wanted a brother and now that he knew he had two younger brothers, he had to find them. Just as he was about to pour more milk into his bowl, his phone rang.

"Hello?"

It was Michael; he knew Richmond was upset the last time they spoke. "Rich, how are you? I have been worried about you since our last conversation. How are you feeling?"

"I'm better," Rich said, as he took in a spoonful of the sugary cereal.

"I spoke with Mom this morning and she told me you have a brother that should be thirty-five or thirty-six years old named Marcus Davenport and a younger brother named Isaac Davenport that should be about three years younger than Marcus. Mom found out that Marcus was raised in foster care while Isaac was sent to an orphanage. However, she said both are living in Georgia."

Richmond almost choked on his cereal. When he cleared his throat, he said, "Michael, thank you man; you are a lifesaver. And tell your mom she should think about switching professions."

Both men chuckled as they released the call. A weight had been lifted from Richmond's shoulders. It seemed he was the only one of the three orphaned children to be adopted. He knew with this information, he would find his brothers and have the family he always dreamed of. As Richmond ate his breakfast he felt peace in his soul and joy in his existence. He stood and walked toward the kitchen counter to put his empty bowl into the dishwater. Feeling pleased with all the enlightening information he had heard, Rich glanced one last time at Melanie's note on the refrigerator. He thought of Cashmere and reminisced over all the events that had taken place in all their lives. He hoped Cashmere would find everything she longed for in her new relationship with Marcus. From what he had noticed and heard Marcus would be a great...

"Marcus," he mumbled. "Marcus..."

In an instant, Rich stopped dead in his tracks and the china bowl he had been holding in his hand shattered onto their tile floor.

Chapter 15

Marcus opened the car door for Cashmere and lifted her body from the car. He carried her, ever so gently, inside her home and laid her down on the living room sofa. Marcus stroked her hair away from her face and held her hands tightly inside his. The passion and love in his eyes was as sweet as honey.

"Cashmere, baby. There's something I need to share with you. I have waited for you since I was thirteen years old. I prayed for you every night. You were always in my dreams. Your face was always with me."

Marcus let go of her hand and slowly pulled out the picture that he kept so sacred in his wallet. Mr. and Mrs. Osborn, Melanie and Olivia watched this sweet episode unfold right before their eyes. They were so happy for Cashmere. The moment was so intense, yet so peaceful; a moment Mr. Osborn had waited on all of his daughter's life. Their eyes and ears were locked on Marcus and Cashmere.

"Cash, I love you. I've loved you and carried you in my spirit for a very long time."

"Marcus, I just want to be sure we are doing the right thing," Cashmere said as she looked for her parents and motioned them to come to her side.

"Cash, baby, let me explain. I went to the fair when I was thirteen years old. There was a lady at the fair who was prophesying. I walked by and she called my name. The lady's name was Margie Alberta," Marcus said, trying to reassure her by rubbing her arms tenderly.

Immediately, Mrs. Osborn's mouth fell open as she placed her hand across her chest, her eyes wide with wonder as she stared at Marcus. Her knees began to tremble as she listened intensely to every word that came from Marcus's mouth.

Marcus continued to address his love for Cashmere, not noticing the reaction from Mrs. Osborn. "She took my hand and instantly started to draw a picture of you. This is the picture right here." Marcus put the picture in Cashmere's hand as he moved closer to cradle her in his arms. "Cash, Margie told me that God had ordained me to love you with an agape love. She said I had been chosen to restore your heart, to fulfill your every emotional need and desire, to appreciate your greatest vision, to cherish you like a precious gemstone and to honor you all the days of my life. She said I would find you in perfect time. Margie also told me to carry this picture in my wallet until the day I have you in my arms. She told me your name would be Cashmere. I had faith in what she said and I believed her."

Mr. Osborn watched tears roll down his daughter's face. He knew in his heart that Marcus would be the perfect man for his baby girl.

"But Daddy," Cashmere said as she looked for his approval, "do you believe this is true?"

Mr. Osborn reached into his pocket and pulled out a picture of Marcus and began explaining the identical scenario to Cashmere. He reminded her of their visit to the fair as well as her losing her memory from her accident. Mrs. Osborn watched in total shock, barely able to believe what she was hearing. She knelt beside Cashmere, took a deep breath and didn't speak for a moment; trying to gather her thoughts and find the right words to say. She knew she had the answer to this love connection puzzle.

CASHMERE CRIES

"Honey, you had a praying grandmother. Cash she prayed for me and you, darling, even before we were ever conceived. I was seventeen years old when your grandmother passed into glory, but I still remember her prayers. She prayed fervently that her family's seed would be blessed. She had an anointing on her life so powerful that she could speak and heal any ailment. Your grandmother's name was Margie Alberta Borders and because she had such an abusive husband, she fasted and prayed to God without ceasing, that God would send loving, spiritual, chosen men into our lives," Mrs. Osborn said as tears welled in her eyes.

Mrs. Osborn revealed that her mother was a gifted artist and had been called to prophetic ministry shortly before her death. As the pictures were compared, there was not a dry eye in the room. The moment was extremely surreal and everyone was touched by the love that surrounded Cashmere's living room. Olivia held Melanie's hand along with Mr. and Mrs. Osborn as they made a human circle around Marcus and Cashmere. Prayers and songs filled the room as each individual gave thanks to God. It was the fervent affectionate prayer from Mrs. Borders that enabled such a magnificent fantasy to come alive in two deserving souls.

As the sounds of worship began to fade, Marcus wondered if Mrs. Borders who lived down the street was related to Mrs. Osborn's family. Though nothing was promising, he felt that maybe his neighbor and Mrs. Osborn were possibly related. Marcus took his arms from the cradling position where he had been holding Cashmere and stood in the center of the room. His eyes locked with Cashmere's mother's eyes.

"There is a lady that lives down the street by the name of Mrs. Borders. Do you think you two may be related?" Marcus asked as he crossed his arm over his chest and scratched his head.

Mrs. Osborn nodded. "It is a possibility."

"Then let's go find out," Marcus said with a huge smile as he reached for her hand.

Mr. Osborn, Olivia and Melanie decided to remain inside with Cashmere and reminisce over all the excitement. Once outside, Marcus led Mrs. Osborn down the side walk. He pointed out to her his home and discussed with her his dreams for a family. He told her about his life in foster care and vowed never to abandon his children the way his parents had done him. Marcus expressed love for Cashmere in words parallel to Mr. Osborn's love for his wife.

All of a sudden, Marcus stopped and looked around as if he were in a strange place. *Where could it be*, he wondered, as he turned around in a circle, and then did the same counterclockwise. Marcus sat down on the sidewalk and rested his face inside his hands. *Was I talking so much that I passed the house?* He considered the impossibility as he looked up the street then down again.

"I can't seem to locate her house. It was just diagonal from my address. But that's a totally different house," he said, pointing across the street. "Mrs. Borders' house seems to have just disappeared."

Mrs. Osborn put her hand on her hips and bit her bottom lip, "Are you sure, Marcus?"

"Yes, I am positively sure. I spoke to her the same day Cash went to the hospital. She told me that Cash's SUV had been parked outside for over an hour with the door open. In fact, she told me to go make sure everything was okay. She was right here," Marcus said, pointing to the exact place where Mrs. Borders had been standing that day, walking her dog.

"This all seems a little too strange, Marcus. An entire house cannot just disappear in mid-air."

Just as Marcus leaned back on the sidewalk, a young teenaged boy approached, delivering newspapers on his bike. Marcus assumed that the paperboy delivered to Mrs. Borders address or at least had seen her walking her dog in the neighborhood.

"Excuse me," Marcus said standing to his feet while straightening his clothes, "do you deliver to Mrs. Borders?"

The paperboy jumped from his bike and let down the kick stand. "Are you talking about the old lady that always wears a white knit bonnet and a pink and white dress and walks an old dog?" the boy asked in one breath.

Marcus nodded, staring at the house across from his. "Yes, Mrs. Borders, she lives across the street."

The paperboy looked over his shoulder at the house that Marcus was referring to and shook his head. "No. I deliver to Mr. and Mrs. Lumpkin at that house across the street," he said pointing to the three story red brick home. "They are my favorite clients. They give me big tips," he added, smiling.

"Well, do you know where Mrs. Borders lives?" Mrs. Osborn inquired.

"No. But I always have an extra paper left over so I give it to Mrs. Borders whenever I see her walking her dog," he said while climbing back on his bicycle. "For an old lady, she can really draw," he said, tossing his papers over his shoulder and releasing the kick stand.

Marcus and Mrs. Osborn looked at each other.

"What did you say?" Mrs. Osborn walked closer to him and put her hand on his shoulder. "Honey, what did you say?"

The paperboy pulled out a hand drawn picture of an airplane. "She gave it to me one day after I told her I wanted to be an airplane pilot."

"Wow, this is really incredible, man," Marcus said staring at the picture along with staring at Mrs. Osborn.

"Yeah, I know. I've tried telling my parents about Mrs. Borders but it seems as though I'm the only one who has ever seen her besides you. But I'll tell her you are looking for her..." The paperboy's voice faded as he mounted his bike and rode away tossing newspapers into driveways.

Marcus held Mrs. Osborn in his arms, comforting her as she shed tears of joy. She knew that her mother was a loving, caring soul. She also knew her mother's spirit was still alive and had been watching over them all along.

She was painfully aware that her mother had been abused by her father. Mrs. Osborn witnessed countless times her mother crying out for salvation for her husband and child. Even though Mrs. Borders did not have a perfect man, she persistently prayed to God to ordain and choose a man for her daughter and every daughter that would be birthed from her lineage. Mrs. Borders wanted to break the curse that had been a part of her family for generations. She knew God's love and that warm affection gave her strength and power to overcome heartache and forgive so all her daughters' kindred would experience true love. Mrs. Osborn heard her mother's voice speaking to her from the Bible, straight from John 15:9-12. She looked up toward heaven, yielding unto the voice of God.

"As the Father hath loved me, so have I loved you: continue ye in my love. If ye keep my commandments, ye shall abide in my love; even as I have kept my Father's commandments, and abide in his love. These things have I spoken unto you, that my joy might remain in you, and that your joy might be full. This is my commandment, that ye love one another, as I have loved you."

Chapter 16

Olivia sat in the living room of Cashmere's home thinking of how God had manifested His love and blessed her friend. She wanted to support Cashmere in her new relationship, but she also had a lot of new information to disclose. Not knowing exactly how to begin, she twiddled her thumbs, anxiously waiting for the conversation to pause so she could jump in.

When the opportunity finally presented itself, Olivia smiled from ear to ear and said, "I have an announcement to make."

With all eyes immediately locked in her direction, Olivia knew she had everyone's undivided attention.

"A few days ago at Lenox Mall, I participated in V-103's annual talent show and I won!" Olivia squealed as she began jumping up and down.

"That's awesome Olivia," Cashmere said as she looked up and smiled at her friend. "You go girl."

"There's more," Olivia told her audience as she held up an envelope and shook it vigorously from side to side. "I am holding in my hand a one million dollar contract with Gospo Centric Productions!"

Silence invaded the room. Everyone's eyes became very large. All at once, with the exception of Cashmere, who could only bring herself to an upright seated position, all of the friends jumped to their feet and screamed in excitement while hugging Olivia. She received immeasurable hugs and kisses.

"We are so proud of you," Melanie said, tightening her grip around Olivia's waist.

Mr. Osborn agreed. "No one deserves to sing gospel more than you. You have a natural talent."

"Yes, sir; I have waited on this opportunity all my life. I have a chance to sing for God and I'm not turning back. He has blessed me and shown favor unto me and I thank Him for His grace everyday."

"This is so wonderful, we should celebrate," Cashmere suggested in a joyful tone.

"Yeah, let's celebrate, let's have a party," Melanie suggested.

"I'll bring the drinks," Mr. Osborn said.

"I'm so proud of you, Olivia. You deserve to sing and showcase your talent more than anyone I know. You are awesome and now the world will know you're awesome," Cashmere said, pausing to breathe and fight the tears in her eyes. "Sometimes in life we are afraid to take chances. We are afraid to really live and then one day, it's too late. I want you to show the world God's love through your voice. You will be amazed how many lives are changed by your music. You have an awesome opportunity to touch lives. I am so happy for you," Cashmere said as she wiped new tears from her face.

Olivia walked over to sit next to Cashmere on the sofa. "Thank you so much for your support. I love you, girl. Now dry your tears and let's plan this party," Olivia said and clasped her hands together. "Thank you all so much, I love you all."

"Okay, enough of all the love talk. I will host the party at our condo Friday night," Melanie said. "And I'll decorate and buy the cake."

"Cash, all you have to do is show up," Olivia said. "We'll take care of everything; you just focus on getting well soon so you can walk down the aisle." She winked her eye at Mr. Osborn and Melanie as she spoke.

"I saw that and you are not funny," Cashmere said, looking sideways at Olivia.

Olivia laughed at Cashmere's silly facial expression. She was blessed in her life, but as she thought of the hungry, homeless man she'd met at the mall just a few days ago, she sobered. Now was her opportunity to help Isaac. He had been on her mind a lot lately and she wanted to make sure she did everything in her power to assist him in getting back on his feet.

Olivia looked out the window, contemplating how to introduce Isaac into the conversation that had nothing to do with him or his situation. She wondered if Mr. Osborn still remembered Isaac. Olivia had promised Isaac that she would help him, but with Cashmere's illness, everything had been in disarray. Now that Cashmere was home, Olivia figured within herself that now was as good a time as any to concentrate on Isaac and make good on her promise.

"Mr. Osborn, do you remember Isaac, a man that worked for you years ago?" Olivia questioned as she moved closer to him.

"Sure. Isaac Davenport?"

"Yes, sir," Olivia answered with a bright smile, glad that the man hadn't been forgotten.

"Oh, yes, I remember Isaac; he was one of my best drafters. You know him? How's he doing?" Mr. Osborn asked as he went into the kitchen to get something to drink. "Would you ladies care for anything?" he offered.

"Water," Olivia said, following him into the kitchen.

"Me too, Daddy," Cashmere called, looking over her shoulder.

"Same here," Melanie said going outside to look for Marcus and Mrs. Osborn who had been gone long enough to have returned.

Olivia was glad for the privacy that the kitchen provided. She sat at the table and explained to Mr. Osborn, Isaac's current situation. She told him how she bumped into him at Lenox mall and bought him lunch. She told him that Isaac was homeless and without a job. Olivia explained Isaac's desire to travel with the company but for the sake of his marriage he stayed behind. And unfortunately, he could not find a job competitive to his previous salary which caused his home to be foreclosed. She also told Mr. Osborn that Isaac's life had spun out of control and he desperately needed help.

Mr. Osborn held up his hand. "Enough said. Tell Isaac to give me a call."

He took out a business card and placed it in Olivia's hand. "This is my direct line."

"I will give this to him today," Olivia said, smiling like a Cheshire cat.

"Who are you recruiting, Daddy?" Cashmere said as she joined them at the table.

"Isaac Davenport, he worked for me in Atlanta before the company moved to Waikiki."

Cashmere looked back and forth between Olivia and her dad with curiosity in her eyes. "Davenport?" she said, turning her glass up to her lips to drink the water that her father had poured for her, but never delivered. "I wonder if he is related to Marcus."

Chapter 17

Melanie was outside on the front lawn when she closed her eyes and shook her head. She took a deep breath and blew out a mouthful of air. She crossed her hands over her stomach and imagined how it felt to have a baby growing inside her womb. She could not wait to start a family with Rich. It was hard waiting, hoping and dreaming of being pregnant, but Melanie respected Richmond's desire to first find his family.

She smiled as she saw Marcus and Mrs. Osborn heading her way. She grinned even wider when she saw the love of her life pulling up in his black BMW 840 CI. Richmond parked his car, jumped out and ran up to Melanie. His demeanor was like that of a child on Christmas day who had just been delivered tons of gifts from Santa Claus and his reindeers. Richmond was running so fast he nearly tripped over his shoelaces. Melanie looked at her husband's feet as he approached her; it was not like Richmond Miccoli to walk around with his shoelaces untied. Something heavy must be on his mind she thought to herself as he rushed up to her.

"Baby..." Rich said, gasping for air. "What is Marcus's last name?"

"I don't know honey, why are you asking and why are you looking so strange? What's going on?"

"I think I found him," Rich said, huffing and puffing with dancing eyes.

Melanie's face was engulfed with confusion. "Found who?"

"My parents and my brothers."

"Baby, that is great!" Melanie threw her hands around his neck.

Richmond held Melanie as tightly as he could without causing her to stop breathing. "I'm so happy."

"Look at these two lovebirds," Mrs. Osborn said as she motioned for Marcus to take note of the exchange between the embracing couple. "They are so cute."

Richmond and Melanie stopped hugging and looked at each other, knowing their lives would never be the same. Melanie let her hands fall from Richmond's embrace as she turned him slowly toward Marcus, who was now standing only two feet away from them. Richmond looked at Marcus and immediately saw the resemblance. He knew without a shadow of doubt that Marcus was his brother.

Melanie's mouth fell open as she stared at Marcus as though she was meeting him for the first time. To see him beside Richmond truly showed their resemblance. She understood now why she felt comfortable with Marcus from their initial conversation. He was family and had the same gentleness with women as Richmond.

"Melanie?" Mrs. Osborn questioned as she stood beside her. "Honey, are you all right?"

Melanie stood frozen with her mouth still open.

Marcus waved his hand in front of her face. "Is Cash okay?"

"She's...uh...mmm...Uh...fine. Marcus, what is your last name?" Melanie stuttered, still staring at Marcus.

"Davenport. Why?" The confusion in Marcus's voice matched the look on his face.

Richmond could not stand the anticipation. He was on the verge of having a heart attack from the excitement. His palms began to sweat and he could hear his heart beating inside his chest. Richmond took a deep breath and reached out to Marcus. "I think we should go inside."

When the group walked inside the house, Marcus went directly to the kitchen table to check on Cashmere. She knew by the look on their faces something was going on.

"I have some information that I have been researching for a long time," Rich said as he took a seat at the table. With a sweep of his arm, he motioned for everyone standing to join him. When they were all seated, he continued. "I was adopted at birth. For over a year I have been trying to locate my birth parents. I found out that my birth mother's name is Sallie Ann Davenport, born in Vivian, Louisiana. She was a single mother and never married."

Uh-huh," everyone said in unison.

Rich looked at Marcus and took a deep breath. "I believe you are my brother."

One by one, Marcus looked in the eye of those that shared the room with him. He was waiting for someone to yell, *"Gotcha!"* or *"It's a joke!"* but no one budged. Marcus had no idea what to say so he did not say anything. He continued to look at Rich with widened eyes that were filled with questions that he could not form the words to ask.

Richmond saw Marcus's apprehensions and answered the unspoken thoughts. "I found out that I have two brothers whose names are Marcus and Isaac Davenport. William B. Wallis is our father," Rich told Marcus. "I know that you were put in a foster home and Isaac went to an orphanage."

Marcus still did not say a word. He had a face of stone.

"Sallie Davenport had three sons by Mr. Wallis who was a very wealthy man in town," Richmond continued. "He was the mayor in town and one of the deacons at New Hope Baptist Church. He refused to allow his wife to find out any information regarding his affair or his children so each time Ms. Sallie became pregnant, he gave her an ultimatum." Rich paused to clear his throat. It was just enough time for Marcus to gain a sense of reality and speak.

"What was the ultimatum?"

"She had to disown us at birth," Rich said, fighting back tears.

Marcus could not fathom what was going on. He could not begin to understand the miracle that unfolded in front of him.

"Oh my God...oh my God...this is so amazing," Olivia said as she looked at Mr. Osborn and then at Richmond and Marcus. As unkempt as he had been when she met him, Olivia could see the resemblance in Isaac and she knew she had the last piece of the missing puzzle. Olivia was so excited she had to stand up. "You guys are not going to believe this. When I was at Lenox Mall..."

"Yeah, yeah we already know about the music deal," Melanie interjected. "Let Rich finish his story and then we'll tell them about the contract."

"No, no. I wasn't going to say anything about the contract," Olivia countered, "just let me finish."

"Go on Olivia, we're listening," Cashmere said, frowning at Melanie.

"When I was at Lenox Mall a guy came up to me and asked me if I could spare some change. I only had my debit card so I offered to buy his lunch. We sat down and talked..." Olivia said as she sat down again staring at Rich and Marcus. "He told me that his name was Isaac Davenport and that he grew up in an orphanage."

"No way," Rich said as he leaned in closer to Olivia and grabbed his chest. "I cannot believe my ears. Please tell me more, tell me all you know," Richmond urged with renewed excitement in his eyes.

"Well, he said he was thirty-three years old, born in Louisiana and raised most of his life in an orphanage. He said that after he finished high school he joined the Job Corp in Morganfield, Kentucky where he got a degree in drafting. He was married to a girl name Wynette but now they're divorced. He used to draw buildings with Mr. Osborn's company."

"Oh man, this is too much for me to digest," Rich said as he held his head in his hands. "I am completely and utterly overwhelmed."

Melanie reached over and wrapped her arm around her husband. After the crying spell that he went through last night, he deserved the good news that today had brought.

"Isaac is homeless and he needs our help," Olivia told them. "He has accepted Jesus Christ into his life but he needs our love and support."

"You should invite him to the party," Cashmere suggested. "What do you guys think?"

"I think it's a perfect idea," Mrs. Osborn replied.

"Me too," Melanie agreed.

Mr. Osborn nodded in agreement while Marcus and Rich shook their heads yes and leaned against the backs of their chairs.

"Great. I'll call Isaac and let him know he's invited to a party," Olivia said, reaching for her purse. She fished around inside until she found her address book. She pulled it out and flipped to the page where Isaac's name had been written. She copied the information down and gave it to Rich and Marcus for their records. It was Isaac's room number at the Hyatt in downtown Atlanta. Olivia had taken him there the day she met him at Lenox Mall and had paid for a thirty-day stay. In that time, she planned to help Isaac re-establish his life. Olivia knew in her heart that God had intervened and answered her prayers. She looked back and forth between Rich and Marcus and their facial expression said a million words. Their lives, which had been separate for so long, were finally coming together all at once.

Chapter 18

Isaac had isolated himself inside his hotel room for days. He had been fasting and crying out for God to answer questions he had regarding his life; especially his childhood. He wanted God to heal him from the hurt he felt growing up as a child abandoned by his parents. Isaac wanted to erase all of the horrible memories the orphanage had embedded in his mind. He prayed that God would take control of his thoughts and free him from the hatred he had for his parents.

For hours, Isaac cried nonstop as he travailed for God to mend his heart and repair his emotional scars. He had cried so hard that his mouth opened but no words formed. Isaac cried himself to sleep many nights holding the complimentary Bible that the hotel placed in the drawer of the nightstand. Isaac did not learn much about God in the orphanage; however, he had knowledge of the 23rd Psalm. As he sat on the side of his bed, he flipped through the Bible until he came across the comforting scripture.

"He restoreth my soul: he leadeth me in the paths of righteous for his name's sake." Isaac read and repeated the words of the third verse until he felt peace in his heart, mind and soul. When he was done, Isaac rose to his feet and stretched out his hands toward heaven and prayed. "Dear Heavenly Father, I put all my trust in thee, I stretch forth my hands and give my spirit unto thee for you have redeemed me. Help me to lift my head and worship thee, for you have turned my sadness into dancing and my cries into praise."

Isaac sat down on the end of the bed and gazed into the mirror in front of him, not even recognizing the face staring back at him. He reached up and touched his face and slowly turned his head from side to side. Isaac stood up and moved closer to the mirror to get a better look at his appearance. It was a terrible sight and he was not pleased. He missed the old Isaac and desperately wanted him back.

A sudden common, but unexpected noise caused Isaac to jump. He turned around, holding his chest to try and slow the beating of his racing heart. It was the ringing of the telephone that had startled him. He walked toward the phone and answered.

"Hello?"

"Hey Isaac, this is Olivia. How are you feeling today?"

"I'm good Olivia, thanks for asking," Isaac responded, mindlessly bouncing the telephone cord up and down as he spoke. "And how are you doing?"

"Oh Isaac, I am wonderful, I am truly blessed and so are you."

"I'm glad to hear that and I just want to thank you again for all of your generosity. You've been extremely nice to me and I truly appreciate you."

"You are more than welcome, Isaac. Have you gone shopping yet?" Olivia asked, hoping to hear him say that he had.

"No, actually I haven't. I've just been lounging around in the robe from the hotel."

He sounds so good, Olivia thought to herself. *He has such a profound sexy voice.* "Isaac, you are invited to a party; please say you'll come," Olivia said, crossing her fingers and trying to do the same with her toes.

"I'll come," Isaac said immediately. "After all you've done for me there's absolutely nothing I would not do for you."

"Okay, I'll pick you up Friday at seven o'clock sharp."

"I'll be waiting," he said, smiling.

"Great. I'll see you Friday, and Isaac, dress casual."

"I can handle that," Isaac said smoothly. "What are we celebrating?"

"It's a surprise," Olivia pronounced in a singing voice.

Isaac, being satisfied with that information, said good-bye and released the call with a smile on his face. Walking across the room, he sat down at the table that overlooked Peachtree Street. He leaned back against his chair and looked at the money that lay on the table in front of him. Olivia had given him fifteen hundred dollars to buy clothes, shoes, hygiene items and his own personal Bible. At the time, Isaac had been overwhelmed and did not know where to begin; but he knew it was time for a change.

Putting the money in his pocket, Isaac headed for the door. He took the elevator to the hotel lobby and passed through the glass doors. Outside on Peachtree Street, he took a deep breath and walked toward Mo'naes Barber Shop. Isaac pushed opened the door and stepped inside. Closing it, he heard a small bell ring above his head.

"Hi, welcome to Mo'naes," the receptionist said from behind the counter. "Do you have an appointment or are you a walk-in?" She scanned Isaac from head to toe.

"I'm a walk-in," he said, looking around the shop.

"Okay. If you'd like to have a seat, we'll be with you shortly," she said as she pranced to the back of the barber shop. She returned shortly with a container of bottled water and a copy of the latest issue of *Essence* magazine. Isaac flipped through the pages trying to find something interesting to read when he noticed an article on Osborn's Construction Company.

"Sir, we're ready for you," the receptionist called, taking his attention away from the article he wanted to read. Isaac stood up clutching his water bottle and magazine as she escorted him back to the available barber.

"What's up man; I'm Anthony." The barber introduced himself and extended his hand. "What can I do for you today?"

"Give me a low cut fade, trim my hairline and touch up my mustache," Isaac said, looking in the mirror.

"You got it," Anthony said, pumping up the chair with his foot.

The barber definitely had his work cut out for him, but he sounded confident that he could do the job. Isaac closed his eyes and relaxed as Anthony draped a cape around his neck. He heard all the noise of barber clippers and men talking about women and cars as usual, but Isaac kept his mind focused on the awesome work God had performed in his life. He decided to just sit quietly without joining the conversation. Isaac was there for one thing and one thing only: a fresh cut.

After several minutes, Isaac felt Anthony nudge him on the shoulder as he unsnapped his cape and shook Isaac's hair on the floor.

"You're all done," Anthony said, turning Isaac's chair so that he faced the mirror. "That's you, playa," he added, grabbing a handheld mirror from the wall next to his station so that Isaac could view his new look from all angles.

Isaac did not recognize himself. Anthony had done the work of a masterful professional. To some, a haircut may have meant nothing, but for Isaac, it was a major makeover that gave his self esteemed a much-needed lift and made him feel good about himself for the first time in years.

"Thanks man," Isaac said, giving Anthony his props and still gazing in the mirror.

The receptionist's expression applauded Isaac's new look as she escorted him to the front of the barber shop where he paid for his hair cut and left Anthony a handsome tip.

"Do you mind if I take this magazine with me?" Isaac asked, holding the periodical up for her to see.

She shook her head and flashed a sly grin. "Not at all, we get so many magazines, I'm sure no one will miss that one."

"Cool," Isaac said, folding the magazine under his arm and taking in stride her lingering gaze of approval.

"Thank you for doing business with Mo'naes sir, have a nice day," the receptionist said as she gave Isaac his change.

"Thank you," Isaac said, smiling as he opened the door and walked toward Macy's to continue his mission.

Chapter 19

Isaac followed the saleslady through the aisle of the men's department at Macy's, noticing all the latest fashions and reaching out to feel the garments that hung on the racks as he passed by. "These are our latest arrivals," she said, pointing to the new Sean John collection. It was exactly what Isaac was looking for. He looked through a rack of jeans until he found his size. He selected five pairs of jeans with matching shirts. Isaac also purchased underwear, socks and shoes, along with two nice leather belts, one brown and one black.

He paid for his items and went directly to the fragrance counter to shop for men's cologne. Isaac smelled so many types of fragrances that he had to take a break between each selection to regain a clear sense of smell. He finally decided on PS, a popular scent by Paul Sebastian.

All the representatives in the store that had assisted Isaac on his shopping spree were female, and a few of them had been bold enough to offer him their phone numbers. It was flattering, but Isaac was not interested. He was a man that loved to be the man. He did not like women chasing him; he wanted to be the pursuer.

Leaving the store, Isaac crossed Peachtree Street and headed back to the Hyatt. Once he was inside his room, he took inventory of his purchases and was satisfied with his choices.

Isaac wanted to call Olivia, but he decided to surprise her instead.

❋ ❋ ❋ ❋ ❋

Marcus could not wait to spend time alone with Cashmere. He parked his vehicle, walked to the door, rang the doorbell and stepped back in wait of her answer.

"Hello beautiful," Marcus said, as soon as Cashmere made her appearance at the front door.

"Hello yourself."

"These are for you." He handed her a dozen red roses, accessorized with greenery and baby breath.

"Thank you so much; they're lovely, Marcus."

"Just like you, baby."

"Let me put these in water, then we can leave," Cashmere said, turning to walk inside.

Marcus followed close behind her. He'd always known Cashmere was gorgeous, but she looked especially lovely today. Her skin was glowing and her hair looked flawless. He noticed music, *Always and Forever* by Heatwave, playing in the background.

"Can I have this dance?" Marcus asked, walking toward Cashmere with his arms open wide.

Cashmere did not answer with her mouth but her actions were loud and clear. She fell into his arms and slow danced to one love song after the other. They were so caught up in the moment that neither one of them noticed an hour had passed.

"I love you so much," Marcus confessed. "I can't wait to wake up to you everyday of my life."

"You mean that, Marcus?"

"With everything within me," Marcus whispered, staring into her eyes. "Baby, trust me, don't let your heart be troubled. I will love you until I take my last breath."

The ride to their destination was void of much talking, but full of admiring glances toward one another. Once they arrived, Marcus walked around to the passenger side of his Mercedes Benz 600 and opened the car door for Cashmere, reaching for her hand to help her exit.

He is such a gentleman, she thought to herself.

Standing in front of the Sundial, Marcus placed his arm around her waist and escorted her inside like a princess. They enjoyed their meals and the conversation between them was nonstop, chatting about everything from politics to reality TV shows. The two found out that they had many things in common such as Dr. Pepper being their favorite drink to the same vision for a Christian family. As the exchange of information continued, they realized they were born on the same day; however, Marcus was ten years Cashmere's senior.

For the next few days that followed, Marcus wined and dined Cashmere, taking her to her favorite dining spots. They visited Pappadeaux, Rudolph's, Luna's and Little Gardens. Her romantic rendezvous with Marcus had been so much fun that Cashmere had actually forgotten about her morbid past. He was everything in a man that Cashmere had dreamed of. Marcus was kind, gentle, affectionate and loving. He loved God and he loved being a Christian. Marcus had given her every detail of his life. She honored him for keeping his virginity, an accomplishment and value that she thought was amazing. Words could not express the gratitude she felt in knowing his body had been preserved for only her.

Although it was embarrassing and painful, Cashmere told Marcus every detail of her marriage to Donovan. He listened carefully and when she finished speaking, he reached over and embraced her.

"Cash, a man has to be a fool not to cherish you. I'm going to love you beyond measure until the end of time."

"Marcus, you are so sweet. I'm so glad I had a praying grandmother."

"So am I baby, so am I."

Marcus walked Cash to her door. Due to the lateness of the hour, he decided not to ask to come in. He gave her a long hug and stared deep into her eyes under the moonlit sky. He felt uneasy in his spirit and knew Cashmere still had unanswered questioned. "Baby, what's on your mind?" Marcus asked, still gazing.

"It's nothing; I had a great time tonight."

"Baby, our souls are connected. I know when something is bothering you. Please share it with me, trust me."

Cashmere loved that Marcus was so in tune with her emotions. It felt wonderful to be understood by a man. "Marcus, I've heard rumors in town. Rumors about your sexuality...rumors that you are gay."

Marcus looked deeper into Cashmere's eyes and pulled her body close to his. "Cashmere, I love you, but more importantly, I love God. My body is sacred, a temple of the Holy Ghost and I would never defile His name. Jesus shed His blood for me. I reverence God for the price He paid for me and therefore I honor my body." Marcus stepped away from Cashmere, but continued speaking. "I want to be all the man you've ever dreamed of. Cash, I take care of my hands and nails for you. When we are married, I want to massage you and caress your body and I want these hands to feel pleasurable to you. I want to feed you dinner at night and strawberries by candlelight. Baby, my manicures and pedicures are for you so you will welcome my touch."

"Marcus, I'm sorry I should ha..."

Marcus placed a finger over Cashmere's mouth. "Baby, don't apologize. I want you to come to me if something is bothering you, no matter how big or small."

Cashmere believed Marcus and she trusted him with her heart but she had to know one last thing. "Marcus, with all the different names in the world, why did you name your florist Beautiful Soft Touch? Most guys would not pick such a feminine phrase."

108

"Most guys don't have Cashmere either," he said, smiling.

"I don't understand."

"Cashmere fabrics are beautiful and luxurious in appearance and are soft to the touch and require special care. Beautiful Soft Touch is named after you."

Tears flowed down her face, one teardrop after the next. She was so overwhelmed by Marcus's words that she could not speak.

"Goodnight precious," he whispered as he kissed the back of her hand. Marcus slid the keys out of Cashmere's hand and unlocked the door for her. "I love you. Sweet dreams."

Chapter 20

Melanie had just placed the cake on the table when she heard the doorbell ring. She quickly headed for the door, stopping by the mirror in the foyer to check her makeup. She'd had company at her house on many occasions but tonight was different. It was a celebration of her life with Rich and their life to come.

"Hey, come on in," Melanie said, standing back to let Mr. and Mrs. Osborn inside. "You can set the drinks behind the bar," Melanie said, pointing him in the right direction. "Rich will be out in a minute. He's so nervous that I don't think he slept at all last night."

"He'll be fine once everyone arrives. You decorated so nicely, the welcome home and congratulations signs are perfect," Mrs. Osborn said admiring the decorations in the room.

Melanie had purchased two huge signs from Party City. One read: CONGRATULATIONS OLIVIA and another said: WELCOME HOME RICH, MARCUS & ISAAC. She had bouquets of balloons in every corner and curly ribbons that hung from the ceiling.

"Rich, how are you?" Mr. Osborn asked as Richmond entered the room.

"I'm good, just anxious," Rich said as he sat down next to Mr. Osborn on the sofa.

"I'll get it," Melanie said as she heard the doorbell. She smiled while opening the door, hoping it would be Marcus and Cashmere; and it was.

"Hey girl, you look so nice," Melanie complimented Cashmere as she reached out to embrace her. Then she turned to greet Marcus as well. "How are you doing, Marcus?"

"I'm fine," he said. "I'm on top of the world."

❊ ❊ ❊ ❊ ❊

Olivia pulled into the parking lot at the Hyatt and called Isaac's room. He did not answer so she dialed the number a second time. When she still didn't get an answer, Olivia decided to walk to his room to check on him.

The glass doors automatically opened for her to enter into the lobby. She was about to push the elevator button when she realized she was early and Isaac could be in the restroom getting ready, which would have made it difficult for him to answer the phone when she called earlier and would make it both difficult and awkward for him to answer her knock at his door.

"I'll just wait until seven o'clock and call again," Olivia said, looking down at her watch. She walked across the lobby and sat down in the waiting area. She could not believe how God had blessed her and her friend. God had chosen Marcus for Cashmere before they were conceived in their mothers' wombs. He had ordained Cashmere's grandmother, Margie Alberta, to be their guardian angel and to intervene in their lives. God had predestined their love and Cashmere's parents' love at her grandmother's prayer request. In the midst of the blessings, God knew that Marcus would need to be whole in order to love Cashmere to the best of his ability. Therefore, He specifically designed Richmond, Marcus and Isaac to reunite at this special point in time. Olivia was so caught up in God's awesome work that she did not notice the man that stood beside her.

"Hello, are you waiting for someone?" Isaac asked, putting his hand on Olivia's shoulder.

"Yes, I'm waiting on a friend," Olivia said, glancing down at his hand, then allowing her eyes to travel up his arm and to his face. She stood up, looking intently at Isaac's face and then backed away from him with her hands over her mouth. "Isaac?" she asked with widened eyes. "Is that you?"

"Surprise!" he said with his arms extended outward so that she could see all of him. He turned around and struck a model's pose. "So, what do you think?"

"Isaac. Isaac. Isaac. You look incredible!" Olivia screamed while staring at him, shaking her head in amazement at his transformation, and eyeing him from head to toe.

He was well over six feet tall with coffee colored skin, most of which had been hidden by the mass of hair that was on his face when they first met. His hair had been cut low and his facial hair had been trimmed to accent his features. He was dressed as if he had just stepped out of a catalog and he smelled unbelievably good. Isaac looked like a new man, he looked better than new money. She automatically noticed the resemblance to Richmond and Marcus.

On the way to Melanie's condo, Isaac told Olivia about his shopping spree and about all the ladies that attempted to flirt with him. He told her that he intended to practice celibacy until God sent him a mate. He was focused on restoring his life and building a relationship with God. To be quite honest, he'd said, a woman was the furthest thing from his mind.

"I really want to thank you for everything you have done for me. I really do appreciate it, Olivia," Isaac said, opening the car door for her to exit as they arrived at Melanie's.

"Isaac, you are welcome. Everyone deserves a new start in life when the devil comes along and steals our joy," Olivia replied as she reached out to accept his hand.

"I am so grateful to have met you," Isaac announced.

"Isaac, the surprise that I was telling you about is waiting on you inside those doors," Olivia said, pointing to Melanie's condo. "You have two very important people that want to meet you."

"What?" Isaac inquired. "Who wants to meet me?"

"It's a small world, Isaac," Olivia said, knocking on Melanie's door. "Especially when it comes to family."

"Family?" Isaac questioned. "I don't have any family. Remember, I was raised in an orphanage."

"Isaac, have you ever wondered if you had any...?"

"Hey girl, come on in," Melanie said as the door swung open. "We have been anticipating your arrival."

Melanie did not have to announce their arrival as the room was suddenly quiet at their appearance. Rich and Marcus stood up and walked toward Isaac with opened arms and tears in their eyes. Words could not express the happiness that filled each person in the room as they watched the brothers embrace. It was a magical experience to see how God had transformed their lives. The scene before them brought truth to the Christian saying of *God may not come when you want Him but He's always on time.*

"Isaac, these are your brothers," Olivia whispered.

Rich and Marcus led a visibly stunned Isaac into the living room where they each brought him up to speed on how they were all separated and now united. Rich told Isaac how he had searched for his blood family for over a year. He told him about all the trials and tribulations he had encountered in searching for them. After Rich told Isaac about his adoption and growing up in the Miccoli household, Marcus shared his testimony of growing up in foster care not knowing anything about his family until a few days ago. He told Isaac that God had been his key to a successful future and God and his son Jesus had been the only family he ever knew.

Isaac could not believe what he was hearing. This was indeed the happiest moment in his life. He had never felt so warm and welcome. God had blessed him with a new beginning and restored his soul. In the presence of his brothers, he felt like the prodigal son being welcomed to a celebration in honor of his return home.

Chapter 21

One Year Later...

Today is the day, Cashmere whispered within herself as Wendy finished styling her hair.

It was November 29th, Cashmere and Marcus's wedding day as well as Mrs. Osborn's birthday. The sanctuary of Glory Tabernacle was decorated with a tropical Hawaiian theme. There were palm trees on the ends of every pew and two on the center stage. Sea shells enclosed in sheer material draped along the pews next to the aisle. Tropical colored floral arrangements lined the stage area and there were hundreds of candles displayed all over the sanctuary. Three one hundred gallon aquariums filled with tropical fish completed the ambience. It was a beautiful unique scene in honor of Cashmere's parents. She knew how much Mrs. Osborn loved Hawaii and she wanted to incorporate her mother's passion on this very special day.

"You are one beautiful bride," Wendy announced as she placed the veil on Cashmere's head. "You look absolutely exquisite."

"Thank you," Cashmere replied as she looked in the mirror, admiring her existence of life.

"Cash, are you ready?" Melanie asked, peeking inside the bridal chambers.

"I've waited on this day all my life, of course I'm ready." Standing, Cashmere walked into the foyer. Her eyes lit up as she watched the ceremony on the wall mounted screen. She could see that the pews were packed to capacity. Marcus, dressed in a white tuxedo, stood beside Bishop J.T. MacFields while Richmond and Isaac, serving as his groomsmen, wore black tuxedos.

Marcus looks like a king, Cashmere thought. *And here comes your queen, baby.*

The ceremony began with Olivia singing *The Lord's Prayer* as the dance ministry floated artistically across the stage, dressed in Hawaiian attire. Taylor and Melanie stood in their respective places as Mrs. Osborn was escorted to the first pew.

"You are the prettiest bride I've ever since in my life," Mr. Osborn whispered to Cashmere. "Besides your mom, of course."

Cashmere laughed at her father's remark. "I love you, Daddy," she said, planting a big kiss on his cheek.

"I love you too, Cash. All I ever wanted was for you to be happy," he said trying to fight back the tears in his eyes.

"Oh Daddy, I *am* happy. I love you so much."

"You have my blessing baby girl, now go and make me some beautiful grandchildren."

"I will, Daddy, lots of them."

"You know what?"

"What?" Cashmere inquired while looking at her father, awaiting his reply.

"You are truly blessed. I prayed and prayed and prayed that God would heal you and He did. When you went back to the doctor, he said it was a miracle that all the tumors were gone."

"The miracle happened years ago, Daddy, when Jesus died on the cross," Cashmere said, interlocking arms with her father's. "We have all power if we only believe. I cried out to God, Daddy, and He heard my cries."

The doors of the church opened and together, Cashmere and Mr. Osborn began to walk down the aisle. Marcus stood at the front of the aisle and sang to his bride as she walked toward him.

It was a beautiful love song that he wrote especially for Cashmere. It was wholesome, sweet and unique. The ushers were distributing Kleenex and fans while Marcus continued the serenade that started the domino flow of tears. He had such an anointed voice that even some of the men in the church were becoming emotional.

"The couple has decided to exchange vows that they have written themselves," Bishop J.T. MacFields announced as he stood between Marcus and Cashmere. "I see how Marcus attracted this young woman, he sung to her," he teased, causing a chuckle to race through the congregation.

Marcus looked Cashmere in the eyes and then, to her surprise, he kneeled on one knee. "Cashmere, my love, my life, my queen and my destiny, I have dreamed of this moment for a very long time. I kneel before you this day with a clean heart, mind, body and soul. I pledge to you my love for eternity. I give you all of me; withholding nothing. I will respect you, cherish you, acknowledge you and honor you as my wife until the day I take my last breath. I promise to support your dreams and protect your heart. I stand before God today and commit my vows to you. I promise to be faithful to you only and I guarantee you my everlasting love."

Cashmere gazed into the soul of Marcus as he held her trembling hands. "Marcus, my love, my hero, my partner and my king; I have dreamed of this moment for a long time. My heart is filled with love and joy because you came into my life. I thank God for sending you my way. I pledge to love you, respect you and honor you. I promise to stand beside you in good times and bad. I will support your vision for our family and reverence your goals and dreams for our household. I promise to be loyal and devoted to you all the days of my life. I will love you with words, actions, devotion and grace."

When the vows ended, Bishop MacFields prayed for Marcus and Cashmere, asking God to bless their union and guide their new path.

CASHMERE CRIES

"Marcus and Cashmere," the Bishop called out, his voice booming over the speaker system. "I pronounce you man and wife. Marcus, you may salute your bride."

The crowd rose to their feet in a standing ovation as Marcus tossed a mint in his mouth, lifted Cashmere's veil and planted a passionate, enduring kiss on her lips. His knees almost collapsed under the emotional high of his very first kiss. Marcus had waited all his life to touch the warmth of Cashmere's lips and the result was well worth the wait. Nothing he ever experienced in his life compared to receiving his first kiss at the altar.

Marcus heard the exit music and he heard the congregation cheering but he was engulfed with his precious gift from God. He held Cashmere in his arms as though he was holding on for dear life. He gave God all the praise. God had entrusted Him with her heart and as long as he had life within him, Cashmere would never have to cry.

Carmita Daniels

CASHMERE CRIES

ORDER FORM

If you would like to order more copies of this title (via mail), please complete the form below and send with check or money order **payable to Carmita Daniels** to the address provided below.

Name: _____

Address: _____

City: _____ State: _____ Zip: _____

Email : _____

"Cashmere Cries"   #Bks _____ x $14.95 = $ _____

GA residents add 7% sales tax ($1.05 per book) $ _____

Add shipping & handling as indicated:
$2.00 first book. $1.00 each additional book $ _____

Total amount enclosed $ _____

**Books ship immediately upon payment clearance unless temporarily out of stock. There is a $35.00 service fee on ALL returned checks.

Remittance Address:

Carmita Daniels
P.O. Box 7385
Chestnut Mtn., GA 30502

Carmita Daniels